David Veronese was born in Chicago. He now lives in
Washington D.C. where he owns an art gallery. *Jana* is his
first book.

JANA
(A Tale of Decadence)

David Veronese

To DERAN:
Another torqued up beatified
consciousness in this
everyday world...
        Yours,
        David Veronese

5/10/94

SERPENT'S
TAIL

Library of Congress Catalog Card No. 93-84270

A CIP catalogue record for this book is available from the
British Library on request

First published in 1993 by Serpent's Tail, 4 Blackstock
Mews, London N4,
and 401 West Broadway #1, New York, NY 10012

Imageset in 10/12 New Aster by Image Setters Ltd,
London EC1
Printed in the United States of America

for eva & amiri

A paranoid is a man in full possession of the facts.
—attributed to Camus

Take heed of loving me,
At least remember I forbade it thee
—John Donne

PART I

It seems like a thousand years ago that I first met Jana. It was at the Bar Europa, a smoke-filled, turn-of-the-century place a few steps off the Leidsestraat in downtown Amsterdam. It was winter and very cold; the air inside was thick with the smell of coffee and hashish.

I must have cut a rather furtive figure. I wore very dark glasses, unsuitable for indoor use, and a tattered knee-length fur coat that I'd picked up in the flea market for seventy guilders. My hair was long and ungroomed, down past the shoulders, and I sported a small turquoise earring in either lobe. I was bent over a jukebox, a large snifter of brandy in one hand, the other traveling the glass atop the machine, reviewing the playlist.

A woman came up next to me. I could smell her perfume; it cut through the heavy air like the sword Excalibur. She set her hand down on the glass, a few inches from my own, and cleared her throat. I felt something wheezing in my heart.

From the corner of my eye I could see an arm wrapped up in a black leather gauntlet. Two or three silver rings were slipped over each finger, and a red silk ribbon was tied around the wrist.

She tapped her thumb nervously against the glass, then stopped. The air between us vibrated and thickened with silence. I stared at the names of the songs until they blurred.

She lifted away her hand and began to laugh. I turned to look at her. She was dressed entirely in ink-black leather; the collar of her jacket was pushed up against her neck like a sailor's, and the gauntlets flared up in stove-pipes past the elbows. Her eyes were painted pitch-dark with shadow, and her hair was as white as the oxide of zinc, thoroughly bleached and ironed flat, so that the ends lay in a sharp line over her shoulders. Her mouth was coarse, with thick lips, her cheekbones were wide and smooth. She was a fair-sized girl, and well-apportioned. She began embracing herself and demurely shivering.

"I think my teeth are going to jump out of my mouth," she said in a thick accent, looking straight at me.

"Why's that?"

"It's the cold," she said, "it's crazy; not even the dogs are going in the street." She puffed her cheeks and blew out robustly. "The ground is so hard, they can't bury the dead ones ... the pipes are frozen everywhere."

I looked over her shoulder. A three-pointed chandelier hung from the ceiling, sprinkling her hair with orange light. "Have you tried jumping up and down?" I asked. "That's good for the cold."

She eyed me suspiciously, a grin still stuck to her mouth. Her lashes, teased out and clipped like bat wings, flickered momentarily. "Yes, I tried that once," she said softly. "But I jumped so hard, all my brains fell out on the floor."

We laughed together like old war comrades. She relaxed herself, the shivering stopped; she fluttered her fingertips against her breasts. From somewhere in the distance I heard the chiming of the midday bell. Her smile shortened and disappeared. I didn't know what to say.

"Are you Dutch?" I knew that she wasn't.

"Hi!" she exclaimed. "What do you care about that shit?"

"I want to play a song. I don't understand the titles. I need a translator."

"Those are stupid songs," she said. "Why do you want to play them? Why do you want to know their names?"

I shrugged.

"Those names are nothing," she railed on, "piles of shit. My name is better."

My brow began to twitch. I looked down at her feet. Her shoes were blood red with sharp blue heels. They were studded with scores of tiny rhinestones, and black cardboard bows were glued to the sides. Her ankles were bare, and the toes were open, despite the cold.

I looked up. The chandelier seemed to be swinging. The long dark walls of the bar went on forever, past the tables and down the stairs.

"Well. What's your name then?"

She straightened her shoulders and stood stiffly, hands on her hips, eyes fixed on mine, as if she were the queen of France.

"My name is Jana," she said in a hushed voice. She aspirated gently through her nose and shook her head. "Jana. Jana. That's me. From the north ... from the dark."

I nodded. "Should be easy to remember."

"Remember," she repeated. "Remember." Her face changed and her voice trailed off. Quizzically, she tilted her head; her hands dropped to her sides.

"I remember nothing," she said flatly. "Nothing. Only my name ... Jana. And that it is cold outside ... And that I need a lot of money."

I bought her a drink at the bar; anisette and Coke. The bar was mahogany, forty feet long; a brass footrail ran along the floor. Old bric-a-brac hung from the ceiling, the lighting was dim and offset. The liquor bottles stretched along the wall on mirrored steps, so they appeared to number in the hundreds.

Jana unzipped her gloves and laid them on the counter. She braced her elbows and rested her chin in the cup of her hands. A small dragonfly, green and red, was tattooed on the back of her wrist. She stared into her drink, leagues removed from the world.

"Your voice is American, yes," she said blandly.

"Yeah."

She bit down on her lip and cocked her head towards me. "It was a pity—wasn't it—about John Lennon. Getting murdered like a dog, in your country."

"I know."

She smiled archly and held her cocktail to her cheek. "Do you like to feel the cold of glass?" She tilted back her head and daintily swallowed half the drink. Three silver hoops hung from each of her ears; they jangled when she moved her head.

"What a shock it is — death." She dabbed at her mouth with a cocktail napkin. She looked infinitely sad, like she might start crying. "What is poor John seeing in the moment, when the blood comes out his stomach, his soul flying to paradise, or hell, to wherever it goes. I don't know."

She produced a triangle-shaped compact and studied herself in the looking-glass. She touched up her lips with a fine-pointed brush, applying a lavender paste from a compartment in the box.

"I am feeling death sometimes in my tongue, or smelling it in my nose." She took a parting look in the mirror, then snapped it shut. "If I trip over my feet, and start to fall — yes — I think I can smell it."

She hooked the barstool with her blood-red shoes and bowed her head. Her white hair fell over her eyes. Perhaps the sun had changed its position in the sky, or someone had altered the lights, for the hall seemed darker.

"What's your name?"

"Eddie," I said.

"Eddie? That's a stupid name. Like a man who sells the refrigerators. You don't look like that." She turned her head and looked nervously over her shoulder.

I removed my glasses and wiped off the condensation with my thumb and forefinger. The world grew suddenly bright and blurry, the girl appeared to be a glowing mass. I put them back on.

The bartender was a largish man with short barbed hair, a starched white shirt and small green apron. He walked along the sparsely peopled bar and stopped at the beer spigots. He raised a frosted mug from the icebox below, set it on the drain, and trained a stream of beer into it.

Jana stabbed at the ice cubes in her drink. With her finger, she drew an x on the side of the glass. Her mouth opened slightly and she became still as can be, like a frog ready to strike a fly.

"Eddie," she whispered. Her words seemed to echo. "The world is shit."

"Yes," I said.

The barman picked up a flat wooden spatula. He released the spigot and began skimming off the overflowing foam with short even strokes. Then he let the glass sit, and folded his arms.

"Eddie—you want to love me, don't you."

"What do you mean?"

The barman let more beer from the spigot, then flogged the spume again and again with the knife, stiffening the collar.

Jana set her hand down next to my elbow. It was small, and seemed to quiver. Her fingernails were long and sharpened; each one was painted a different color.

"How much do you pay to sleep with me?"

"I don't know," I said. "A thousand guilders."

"Two thousand."

"Okay."

"Let's see the money."

I took my wallet from its pocket and laid it flat on the bar. It was of plain brown leather, embossed with geometrical forms. My sister had given it to me as a present some months before she shot herself.

Jana prised it open with two fingers and lazily sifted through the bills. She tossed her head and the hoops jingled. Her eyes caught a light from the bar and glittered like a cat's.

"This is only five hundred dollars," she said. She let the wallet fall to the bar. "Do you really think I am a whore?"

"Why should I care?"

She arched her back and splayed her fingers across the counter. The backlights of the bar showed her in silhou-

ette. There was a noise of voices from across the great
hall, but we did not look. She leaned over and lightly put
her hands behind my neck. "You can't have me now,
Eddie," she whispered in my ear. "You're too early. My
price is not in coins."

Her perfume smelled like nirvana and my heart went
into my throat. I had no idea of what to do.

"Look in my eyes, Eddie."

"Okay."

"I'm in trouble. You have to help me."

"Okay."

We walked together down the Leidsestraat. It was high
noon of a cloudy winter day. The sidewalks were jumping
with traffic; people were talking in every which language,
moving quickly to keep warm. A trolley came rattling
down the middle of the street, ringing its bell.

"Come Eddie, you must not walk so slow." Jana let go
of my arm and raced across the tracks, directly in the path
of the streetcar. It missed her by a yard, and she disappeared.

When the tram passed she was briskly walking along
the balustrade on top of the Keizersgracht. I thought
she'd be sloppy on her feet, but there was none of it. She
stood straight as a field marshall and her step was firm
and graceful, like Venus in high heels.

She stopped at the acme of the bridge and leaned
against the railing. She peered into the waters of the
canal. A stiff wind blew up from the south; her flat ironed
hair fluttered like a piece of silk.

I didn't hurry. I looked carefully both ways and crossed
the street. I pushed my way through a thicket of pedestrians struggling to gain entrance to a bookshop. I kicked a
few ankles as I passed.

I stood next to her, resting my elbows atop the parapet
wall. Beneath us in the canal a gondola was moored to a
stone peg in the embankment. A bunch of mallards were
pecking at its hull.

"Poor little ducks," whispered Jana. "They must be so cold, I feel so sorry for them." She put two fingers to her lips, and blew them a kiss. "But also, I am very hungry, and would be happy to eat one—smoked—with orange marmalade sauce."

She leaned far over the rail and put her hand to her brow. She swept her head back and forth, searching the walkway along the canal. A hazy sun appeared from behind the clouds and the water took on a glittering tint.

"There are no other lives, are there, Eddie? Everything is right now—isn't it so?"

"I don't know."

She unzipped a pocket over her breast and took out a slip of paper. She turned around and looked at me, worrying at the paper with her fingers.

"Here is the direction where you must go," she said in a shaky voice. The sun retreated behind the clouds, and the waters behind her darkened. "It is in the Prinsengracht, half a kilometer down, near the Looier, where they are having the antique stores. You know it?"

"I can find it."

"Climb up two stairways and go to the blue door."

She put the note in my hand and embraced me around the rib cage, touching her cheek to mine. She smelt slightly of sweat; its smell mixed curiously with her perfume. I looked at the sharp curve of the canal.

"That is where my friend lives," she said into my ear. "She is very beautiful, Eddie—her hair is very black, her eyes are very green. Italian, she is called Margo Bellini—you will be sure to like it."

She was soft and wonderful to feel in my arms, and I knew that this was not at all on target, correct or decent—but it seemed a million times better than anything else.

"Tell her that Jana sent you, that Jana is all right—that she is safe, away from harm for this moment. She will tell you what to do ... how you can help me."

She pulled back from me, keeping her palms on my shoulders. The wind was gusting and her earrings tinkled like wind chimes. I tried to read her eyes, but the pupils were too large, engulfing the irises like an eclipse.

"Go now. Nothing waits."

I crossed back over the Leidsestraat and walked down a few blocks. I stopped to look through the window of a travel agency. Inside, globes of the world, blue and brownish-green, hung from polished chrome rods, and miniature airplanes, white, with the Dutch flag embossed on their sides, flew around them in tight mechanical orbits. A man sat behind a laminated burgundy desk, typing at an emerald-colored computer terminal.

I turned up the Prinsengracht. It looked about the same as it had in the seventeenth century, when Rembrandt and Hobbema walked these streets. Long winding rows of two- and three-story buildings braced the edges of the canal; capstans and benches—trees boxed in by iron picket—described the walkway, and every few blocks an arching stone bridge spanned the water.

The buildings were very old, but the brick was continually being sandblasted and repainted, creating the look of a life-size Gothic dollhouse. Flowerboxes sat on the windowsills, and ceramic tiles, orange and blue, lemon-yellow and green, were inlaid in the doorways. An iron hook was always set above a bay window of the top floor, in order to raise furniture and carpeting from cargo boats, and winch them into the houses.

Shards of ice bobbed in the water; a gull swooped down, looking for food. I passed a small restaurant and a fruit-and-vegetable stand. There was an art gallery with tiny canvases floating in the window. The building was painted white, with red lacquer trim that had a nearly mirror finish.

I studied Jana's note. It was written in fountain pen; her handwriting was small and exact. I referred the number against the address of the gallery. I walked down fifty feet and arrived at a three-storied stone building.

I walked up some steps. The front entrance was unlocked. I climbed to the landing of the third floor. A window was open down the hall and it smelled cold and clean. The linoleum floor was scrubbed and waxed. I knocked on the door.

A bolt turned, and a man appeared in the doorway. He was tall and immaculately groomed, except for a two-day growth of beard. He wore a black jumpsuit with a white belt and white duck shoes.

"*Ja*. What do you want?"

"Is Margo here?"

His eyes darted back and forth while the rest of him remained perfectly still. "No," he said, "I'm sorry. She is not here right now." He inched back as if he were about to shut the door.

"Jana sent me."

He thought for a moment. His face was stern and he seemed capable of great concentration.

"Come in, please," he said, making a gesture. He snaked his hand around the edge of the door and pulled it open. There was an expensive gold watch on his wrist and his fingers were manicured. "Sit down for a minute. I will be right back with you." He spoke precise textbook English, slightly accented.

He disappeared through a rose curtain hung in a doorway to the right, and I stepped forward into a large room. Three huge bay windows, shutters thrown open, took up most of the wall facing the canal. A long sofa upholstered in gray linen, was set up in the center of the room, so that you could sit and enjoy the view. A low coffee table, raw ash or maple, was placed in front of it, slightly askew. A number of pine bookcases lined the walls.

I sat down at the sofa. On the table were several art books; I recognized a painting by Quentin Massys on one of them. A copy of yesterday's *Le Monde* was spread open next to a porcelain ashtray.

The sun had come out and was glorious over the canal, shining through the winter haze. The ceilings of the room were very high and I felt bathed in light. I thought I heard the distant sound of someone on the telephone.

The man reappeared in the doorway of an adjacent room. He regarded me with a puzzled look. "Something to drink? A beer—or a whiskey, maybe?"

"No, I'm all right," I said. "How about a glass of water?"

"Of course."

He came out with a bottle of Ramlösa and a tall thin frappé glass. He stood over me and poured out half the mineral water. He nudged a coaster emblazoned with a coat of arms across the coffee table and set down the glass on it.

"Cheers."

I nodded. The bubbles danced atop the water. I was not really thirsty.

"You are American."

"Yes."

He sat down a few feet from me and leaned back. He rested his hands at his sides. I noticed a long scar along his neck. "You don't much look it," he said.

"Thank you."

"Do you have dollars?"

Outside, three young girls rode along the canal on their bicycles. They all wore long coats, and identical tall fur hats. A small dog, some kind of terrier, ran after them, barking and jumping at the wheels.

"Why do you ask?"

"Because," he explained, "what Jana wants costs seven hundred Dutch guilders. But I invite you to pay in dollars. Three hundred and fifty."

I looked at the Quentin Massys. A money-changer and his wife were weighing coins on a scale. A convex mirror sat between them facing out at the viewer.

"Isn't the dollar weak now?"

"That's true," he said. "But it always values up sooner or later. Even the Russians can't stop that. I always like to have a few in my purse." He smiled. "Yes. I like the look of them. All the same dull green."

I drank my water. It tasted slightly of salt. I took out my wallet, counted out four hundred-dollar bills and laid them on the table.

"Do you have change?" I said.

He pinched his nose between his thumb and forefinger and released it. I looked at Benjamin Franklin's gouty face and fur-lined collar. "What is your name?" said the man cheerfully, as you would to a child.

"Eddie."

"Eddie—I am called Werner."

"You're not Dutch."

He shook his head. "I am German."

"Do you live here?"

"In Amsterdam? Yes, I do. Many years. I like it."

"Why is that?"

"Short prison time." He started laughing and picked up an opaque beer bottle. He looked at the label and took a long drink, baring sharp white teeth. Then he set down the bottle and sighed.

"Why are you here, Eddie?" he asked. "The hippie times are over now, aren't they?" A red ceramic bowl held an array of brightly wrapped candies. He picked one out and carefully began removing the paper. "But I like your costume. And I like your money." He took a bite out of the chocolate.

"Oh, this is a good one." He smacked his lips. "The Swiss make damn good sweets, don't they? Ever been there?"

"Yes."

"Clean bastards aren't they? It can take a good hour to find the trash can. They're all disguised as trees." He finished the chocolate and sucked off a fleck that had caught on his thumbnail.

"I must go now." In a fluid movement he got to his feet. He was very tall, perhaps six-five. "I have no change for you. I'll bring you back a hundred guilders when I return." He leaned over and swept the bills off the table. He riffled them with his thumb and rubbed them between his palms.

"Yes," he said. "Superior currency. Hard as sandpaper." He folded the bills neatly and slipped them into the hip pocket of his jumpsuit. "I shall be back within the hour."

"I don't understand."

He raised his eyebrows and stared at me. "You don't think we keep it here in the house do you?"

I shrugged my shoulders. I thought of Jana's perfume, and watched the light falling on the windowsill. "It doesn't matter," I said.

Werner pulled on a pair of powder-gray gloves, and stepped past me toward the bookcase. He lifted a great white bear coat off a wooden coat rack and slung it over his shoulder. He saluted me with a finger to the eyebrow, turned, and put his hand on the doorknob.

"Make yourself comfortable, Eddie. There's some sausage in the icebox. I'll be back soon."

I waited for a long time. Through the window, the sun dropped closer to the canal; the tones of the furniture changed, blocks of light moved along the wall.

I fought my way through a few pages of *Le Monde*. I read an article about the Middle East, something about the sudden rise of Islam. Since Mohammed preached in the eighth century, I didn't quite understand. I read some advertisements.

I thumbed through an art book. It was printed in Italy and the reproductions were incredible. There was a picture by the Master of Flanders, in particular, that put the fear in me. I'd never seen it before, and despite the flatness of the page, it appeared three-dimensional. I noted the name of the museum where it hung.

I got hungry. I shut the book and went into the kitchen. It was small and neat as a pin. The walls were gleaming white. They were trimmed top and bottom in delft blue, the molding sanded, buffed and lacquered to a lustrous finish. A butcher block counter was butted to a stainless steel sink, a tiny yellow-orange icebox was wedged beneath it. The floor was made of alternating blue and lemon tiles.

I opened a little drawer and examined the silverware. It was a rather nice Japanese design, a good trademark, but not worth much to the collector. There was a set of china stacked in a glassed-in cabinet above the sink. It was hand painted and well-done, but likewise all too modern to capitalize on in a quick sale.

I took a package of smoked meat and some cheese from the icebox. I made a sandwich with some black bread that was wrapped in waxpaper. I took it and a bottle of Dos Equis and sat down at a square ash table.

On the wall there was a poster of a huge pair of red lips, and a cork bulletin board sprinkled with notes and snapshots. I recognized Jana in one, standing next to an exotic looking dark-haired woman. They were wearing skis and there were mountains behind them. In another picture, the man, Werner, was holding a shotgun in one hand, and a dead rabbit—by the ears—in the other.

After I finished eating, I wiped the counter and table and walked into the bedroom. It was a woman's room with a smell of sachet and perfume. The colors, and everything, were soft; a wave of languor and sleepiness came over me.

I went to the bureau and opened a middle drawer. It was filled with lingerie—beautiful stuff—mauve, pale green and rose-pink, neatly folded, sorted and stacked. The next drawer held trinkets and small jewelry boxes—trays opened, lined with red plush. There was a nice pair of earrings, sterling silver crescents with sapphire baubles pendent at the bottom points—they looked Turkish or Moroccan—I'm not much at gems. I put them in my pocket.

I opened the door of a closet; it smelled of cedar and violets. There was a lovely pair of emerald shoes on the floor. They were perched on spiked black heels and were slightly splayed, as if a real person were standing in them. The clothes hooks were filled with dresses, mostly soft and easy on the eye. A pile of sweaters was stacked in the corner.

I returned to the sitting room. It was nearly dark outside. Bicycles and scooters whirled by along the canal; the workplace was breaking for the day, and all were converging on their short hours of freedom.

A woman came up the walk, the one from the photograph. She was a knockout all right, and I felt slightly dazed, a touch of shock. She wore a tight red sweater, black toreador pants and white cowboy boots. Her hair was piled on top of her head, and she moved very slowly, almost in slow-motion, as if she were walking out of the pages of a book. She held a huge shopping bag in either arm.

I walked out of the apartment and down the stairs to the bottom landing. I pushed my hands into the pockets of my fur and took a deep breath. Margo Bellini was standing just inside the door, opening the mailbox with a key. She removed a number of circulars and a picture postcard. The hall smelled of violets.

"Hi," I said.

She fumbled with her mail and looked at me. Her eyes were very large and dark, and painted with several layers of blue and green on the lids. She had a pronounced nose and her lips were thick and lush with magenta lipstick.

"Hello," she said absent-mindedly. She dropped the circulars into a trash can next to a radiator. Her movements were imperfect. She placed a hand on her hip and looked at the floor.

I opened my mouth and started to say something, but she interrupted me, holding up her hand at eye level. "No, no please," she said. She gasped for breath and flailed her arms. "If you could just help me out for a minute."

I looked at her carefully. Her face was perplexed; she was increasingly flustered. "I am just back from the market. My bags are sitting on the stairs." She let her hands flop against her legs and bent her shoulders. "I am so tired from work—I cannot move anymore." She let out a deep breath. "Please, sir. Will you help me bring them in? They seem to weigh a hundred kilos."

"Sure," I said. "Okay."

"Oh thank you. I know you don't I? Or are you—what do you say—the man on the white horse?" She giggled and smiled a big beautiful one; her eyes were shining. She turned and held open the door for me; I walked out onto the stoop.

The air was cold and brisk, and the streetlights had just come on. I heard the sound of a piano from a flat above. I didn't see any bags and I heard the door slam shut with a bang, and the turning of a lock. I wheeled slowly back around and saw the woman picking up her bags from behind the radiator and disappearing into the darkness of the staircase.

I tested the door. It was quite locked.

I woke up the next day feeling like shit. Begrudgingly, I sat up in my bed and looked through the little window sandwiched between it and the bureau. It was snowing.

The Dutch snow is funny stuff. It sails down in a blizzard for five or ten minutes, then suddenly it stops. It clears up for an hour, maybe two or three—the sun may appear—then it flares up again, blinding everything.

It *was* a very cold winter in Europe, the rooms would never heat up completely. I couldn't imagine leaving my bed. I picked up the phone from the bedside stand and asked if they could bring the breakfast up to me.

I lay flat on my back and pulled the quilt up to my neck. I counted the pink flowers that studded the ivory background of the curtains that bracketed the window. Awkwardly, I reached my hand down beneath the bed and tapped about with my fingers, extracting, at last, a packet of tinfoil from the pocket of my jeans.

I turned on my side, facing the wall. I carefully unwrapped the foil and regarded a slight, jagged shard of black hashish. I raised it reverently between my thumb and forefinger and held it to the light of the window. I placed it beneath my tongue—it tasted bitter, as it must. I chewed it up and swallowed. My throat was too raw to smoke it anymore.

I pulled the pillow over my head. I was very nervous and I wanted it to be dark again. They knocked on the door.

"Come in. It's open."

"Where will I put it, sir?"

"On the bed. Next to my feet—take yourself a guilder from on top of the bureau."

I propped myself up on the pillows and drank some coffee. I reviewed my finances. Minus the four-hundred that I'd made shit sandwiches with the night before—I was left slightly short of a grand. The hotel was cheap, and I could eat meatballs out of the automats on the street for fifty cents a throw; with beer and pin money I'd need about eighty guilders a day, and a return to London. That would leave me about six or seven hundred dollars to invest.

Pieces of life began to come together again, slowly, like that, in an acceptable format. What did it matter about the money blown in the name of love—or lust? I'd give it all to her again, she needn't have used her wiles, she only needed to ask, and I'd be on my knees, reciting all the holy names of God, and throwing the money at her, one, two, five, fifty, one hundred dollars at a time, until I was penniless.

I slathered half a piece of white bread with butter and red jam, ate it, and finished the pot of coffee. I listened to the radiator fighting a losing battle against the cold and licked the last scobs of raspberry from my fingers. I dragged myself out of bed and down the hall to the shower. The water was reasonably warm and the hashish began squeezing me about the kidneys and pushing at the back of my eyeballs.

I put a towel around my waist, gathered up my bit of soap and padded back to my room on the ancient cheap carpet. My glasses were a little fogged, and I drifted back and forth from the parallel world.

I pushed open the door to my room. I never troubled to lock it, it was too much bother to cart around the key.

Jana was sitting on the bed smoking a cigarette. Her feet were propped on the end rail, her back was against the wall. A shot of perfume and steam hit my nose, as if I'd entered a hothouse. A film of sweat raised up above my eyebrows.

I sat down on a chair next to the sink and watched her. She was oblivious it seemed, to everything, her face impassive and emotionless. She was dressed again all in black leather; she sported a royal blue handbag and wore high-heeled shoes that were purple with white polka dots. Her hair was vertically streaked, maroon against the platinum—a shock of it was plaited in the back and pinned up on top. Her lips were painted icy white; she'd meticulously drawn in round her eyes varied colored wedges of mascara, so they looked like wheels. In her hand, she held a cut-glass ashtray.

"I'm sorry what happened, Eddie," she said after some time. She took a drag off the cigarette and allowed the smoke to waft up from her mouth; she inhaled it sharply back through her nostrils and released it in a soft jet from her mouth again. "You should never give this money to Werner, only to Margo."

I tried to pull my fingers back through my wet hair, but it was too rife with knots to get them through. I stood up and went to the bed, stooped and picked up my tattered jeans. I let the towel drop and pulled them on.

I stood over the sink and turned on the water to shave. I checked my teeth in a tarnished silver mirror and lathered my face.

"Nice friends you've got."

I watched her in the mirror. She stubbed out the cigarette in the glass ashtray and scowled. "I can't help it if Margo likes this bastard," she said coldly. "I did not know he would be there. I thought he was still in the jail in Vienna."

"The girl didn't seem too excited to see me, either."

I made a few passes at the lather with the razor. I failed to remember that the blade was new and I drew blood. I winced and shaved over the cut.

"She did not know. She did not know who you were. Everything happened backwards. She was scared—she was afraid." Jana looked in her handbag for another cigarette. "I hope you don't mind when I smoke."

"There's nothing to care about."

"Don't talk to me like this, Eddie."

"Okay."

I cut myself again. The lather turned pinkish. I finished shaving, splashed cold water on my face and wiped myself with a hand towel. I turned and faced Jana. She looked perfect, as if she'd been painted by Botticelli or Rogier van der Weyden. She sat motionless, her arm cocked back past her ear, an unlit cigarette poised between her third and fourth fingers, her face made-up like the wife of pharaoh.

"I brought you back your money."

"Oh, yeah."

"That's right ... don't be so surprised."

"How much?" I hung the towel over the back of the chair. It was covered with red splotches of blood.

"Everything," she said. "What it costs me. Seven-hundred guilder... three hundred and fifty in dollars."

"What do you mean?" I said sharply, acting surprised. "I gave him four hundred."

"No, not the change," answered Jana. "You don't get that back. It's not possible. You need at least something to remind you of being so stupid."

She lay back on the bed, shifting the cigarette to the other hand, then waving it in a circle like a wand. She tapped her heel against the end rail. "Come, Eddie," she said softly. "I'll fix your hair—it looks like the flying mouses have got to it. I'll explain everything to you. Please. Come here."

I pulled on a T-shirt and went to the window. The room

overlooked a courtyard, where several buildings came
together in an irregular rectangle. Each building was lay-
ered with porches, abandoned for the winter. The snow
had stopped falling and the wooden floors and banisters
were dusted with white. I pulled open the window a few
inches.

"I need some fresh air," I said. "Why don't you come
over here?"

I looked at the mirror. At its edge, I saw her rising
slowly from the bed; she removed something from her
purse and held it behind her back. She walked up behind
me on tiptoe, quiet as a panther, and her reflection disappeared. She put one arm around my neck and stuck something into my back.

"Maybe you will die now, Eddie."

"I hope so," I replied.

"You have other girls, don't you, Eddie." She tightened
her grip on my neck and pressed the object harder into
my spine.

"Why do you say that?"

"You don't want me enough."

She pulled the comb out of my back and began unknot-
ting my hair with it. Her fingers felt pleasant against my
scalp; she was very patient, picking at the strands with a
deft touch, and the comb began to pass through. Across
the courtyard, a small bird landed on the railing. I closed
my eyes.

When Jana finished with my hair she let the comb drop
to the floor and held me around the waist. She put her
chin on my shoulder. I opened my eyes and I could see us
cloudily reflected in the pane of the window, vague gray
forms. Jana took a deep breath and sharply exhaled
against my cheek.

"I changed my mind," I said. "I want you."

"I know ... but not enough."

"Well," I said, "then how do I get back the last fifty
bucks. I want that enough."

"Eddie." She laughed. "You are too funny. Take the

money I give you and forget the other. Do you know what Margo and I have to do, to get all this back from Werner? We have to beg. We have to cry. But he gives it ... because it is mine ... because Margo is too upset. He is bad luck, this man, he brings the blackness with him. He says you are a fool. He will never give back the rest. You must leave it."

She slid her hands along my rib cage and stuck the tips of her fingers inside the front of my jeans. I pointed to our murky reflection in the glass. "That's us," I said.

"Some of us," replied Jana.

"Where's the rest?"

She rubbed her nose against my neck. My mouth was dry and something was pounding in my ears.

"The rest of me? It's in a dream or a nightmare—God knows where—it's in a secret box under the ground. I don't know really, I don't remember." She dug her teeth into my neck.

"I don't want you," I said.

She pushed her thumbs against my kidneys. It was maddening. She released her bite. "That's good, Eddie," she said in a low voice, glossed with silk. "Maybe I like that. Wanting is in steps—in degrees—like the temperature in the skies, like the water on the stove." She swept her hands along my ribs and squeezed shut her eyes. "When it comes past boiling, it goes over the pan, and makes out the fire. The fire does not want the water to bubble too hard."

"Okay."

"Lie down on the bed. I make something nice for you."

"Okay."

I washed myself off and got dressed again. Jana stood in front of the mirror and tinkered with her eye make-up, using a tiny brush and a diamond-shaped tin that she had taken from her purse. It was impossible to know what she was thinking about.

"Eddie, I have to use the telephone."

"There's one next to the bed."

She made half a turn from the mirror and looked at the wall. She dropped her hands to her sides. "This phone goes to the office?"

"Yes it does."

"I don't like that." She picked her purse up from the chair and returned the paraphernalia. "My words are private," she said. "No one should be listening."

"I think there's a pay phone in the lobby."

She walked across the room. She held her carriage high and rolled her elbows with each step, as if she were crossing a boulevard. She tucked her bag under her arm and swept the coins on the dresser into her palm.

"I may take some of these for the phone? I haven't anything small." She bowed her head and shrugged her shoulders. "It's okay, Eddie?" she said, her voice tentative and uncertain.

"Sure."

Jana turned and smiled. The world lit up. She crept up to me, sliding her heels on the floor. She stood on her tiptoes and kissed my ear. "You will watch my purse for me."

"Okay."

She crouched and neatly pitched the bag underhand onto the bed. I reached down and grabbed her wrists. I pulled them up and behind her back. She stiffened. "Let go, Eddie," she said sternly.

"How did you find me?" I said.

She tried jerking her arms away. She was surprisingly strong. I lifted her wrists a little higher.

"What do you mean?" she said imperiously, enunciating each word. "This is a stupid question, isn't it? Maybe I don't understand your English. Do you mean how I like you in the bed? I don't answer this question. Never."

"That's not what I mean," I said, not sure what she was up to. I let go of her. "How did you find my hotel?"

She massaged her wrists with her fingers; a rueful look of surprise passed over her face. "Oh, that," she said, seeming to blush. "I'm sorry. Language makes the funny problems."

I folded my arms and waited. She stepped to the side,
touched her hands to her hair and adjusted the pins in her
braid. She turned her head at forty-five degrees and
looked at me over her shoulder, behind the arch of her
arms. "I have a friend in the police," she said calmly. "He
called all the hotels."

I felt a tinge of anxiety; the adrenalin made everything
go slightly out of focus. "What do you mean, Jana?" I said
harshly. "You're mixed up with the police?"

"No, no, no, Eddie. Don't be stupid." She craned her
neck around further in my direction and pushed her fingers up through her hair and held the pose.

"It's just a friend," she continued. "I know him since I
am a little girl." She lowered her hand and turned her face
from me. She'd adjusted her hair so that her neck was
bared. "I don't know. Sometimes it's not so good. He
thinks he is in love with me. It happens this way. I don't
know what it means when someone loves and I cannot
give it back the same way. No one knows."

She turned to me once again. She tilted her head and
stared shamelessly—indignant—her eyes wide open,
hands on her hips. "Don't worry about it," she scolded.
"How the hell else am I going to find you?"

A glaze of sunlight passed in from the window, whiten-
ing the electric glare of the lights in the room. Jana bit on
her small finger and her eyes swept back and forth.

When the door closed behind her, I went for the handbag. I dealt the contents out onto the quilt; there were
exotic lozenge boxes of make-up, vials of nail polish and
long thin tubes of lipstick; wadded tissues smeared with
rainbows. There was a small address book bound in green
leather, a fountain pen, an Italian-made switchblade with
a silver and onyx handle, a faded madras coin purse and a
pearl rosary.

I unclipped the latch on the coin purse and counted fifteen hundred guilders. Then I returned all the items and
set the bag back in its place.

While I waited I sat on the edge of the bed and listened

to the radio. I read a slim pamphlet, a biographical account of Hieronymus Bosch, who, at the end of the fifteenth century, had lived some thirty-five miles from where I sat. They knew little enough about him, he was but briefly mentioned in the church and city records of his town. His wife was landed, and he was supposed to have led a conventional life; he was a member of the Brotherhood of Our Lady. There seems to be a precise superstructure to the thousands of odd unholy scenes in his paintings, but no one can identify the sources of the imagery.

After half an hour, I went out into the hall and rode the elevator down to the lobby. In a glass booth opposite the reception there was a public telephone—a white handset on a square maple shelf. It was not in use.

A flight of winding stairs led to a lounge area in the basement, where they served breakfast. I walked down the stairs. The room was empty, the tables all covered with white cloths and sparkling silverware, primly set for the next day. I looked behind a partition into the kitchen. It was empty.

I walked back up to the lobby. The desk clerk, a young woman dressed in yellow, smiled at me momentarily, then continued with her paperwork. I rode the elevator back upstairs.

The room smelled strongly of Jana's perfume. I looked at the bed for her purse but it was gone.

I went to the window and looked out into the courtyard. It was snowing again, but very weakly; large soft flakes drifted onto the abandoned porches like leaves.

My hotel was on the Jan Luykenstraat, a quiet tree-lined street near the museum district. I walked down the sidewalk, the condensation of my breath trailing me in the cold afternoon. The snow had stopped and a dull sun glared behind the clouds; a thin blanket of white sat on the eaves of the old houses. Across the street, a group of children scrambled back and forth across a schoolyard bounded by a low stone fence.

I walked onto the Museumplein, a wide stretch of park-way that fronted the Asian entrance of the Rijksmuseum. I crossed the street and walked through an archway that led into a tunnel beneath the building. Pictures of griffins and fighting lions were tessellated in the brick. A row of stained-glass windows, the panes blacked by time, stretched out above them; a honeycomb of vaulted arches loomed overhead. A young Arabic-looking man stood at the edge of the walk playing a violin; a pork-pie hat was overturned at his feet.

I emerged through the other end of the passageway, and paid the entrance fee. I gathered my composure and walked painstakingly up the great staircase and along the corridors until I located Vermeer's *Die Kukenmeid*. I stood in front of it, spellbound, amazed to be the only person in the world looking at it at that moment. The painting defied all the conventions of gravity, with the objects in the maid's domain, particularly the golden bread-basket, floating off the canvas and into the room. The light in the work was blinding, and I felt the energy passing through my nerves, hot and cold rising up my back. This is God I thought.

I walked through the white halls. An oriental tour party was gathered around Rembrandt's *Nightwatch*. A con-spicuously tall guide spoke to them in lightning choppy language. I quickly turned the corner, careful not to be distracted by the huge canvas.

Outside again, I crossed the Singelgracht and looked back at the towering building. Two belfries rose up from it into the sky; a golden clock sat between them, two fig-urines holding mallets struck a bell to mark the hour. Above the clock, a strange and frightening creature peeked out at the city.

A flock of gray gulls flew over my head. I looked over the edge of the bridge into the cold waters. A paddle-boat was moored against the stone jetty. I watched a shape form in the brine, then dissolve.

I caught a tram headed eastward. It crossed the canal over the Amstel into the less picturesque part of the town. We sailed past banks and office buildings, then passed along a hundred yards of construction site, the earth ripped open and sprouting lodes of concrete and thick steel girders.

I descended at the Waterlooplein. Cars and buses sped around a traffic circle. There was a blue and white sign advertising a line of diamonds, and another pointing the direction of Anne Frank's house. I wandered around, slightly lost. I took directions in a bar, and finally I chanced upon the grounds of the outdoor flea market. The stalls stretched out for a few city blocks.

I walked up and down the aisles. I passed a stand where they sold old dental tools and another that specialized in washing machines. There were postcard stalls, and booths that had only tiny wooden toys no bigger than your thumb. At a certain table, young men dressed in flowing robes and wearing white scarves around their heads, sat behind a display of cheap jewelry, smoking hashish and tobacco from a Moroccan chillum.

I found the section where clothing was sold. It was hard to tell where one stall began and the other ended. I wended my way through the maze, pulling at cuffs and inspecting hems and pockets. The air was filled with the bitter smell of naphthalene.

I felt a hand on my shoulder. "Well, if it ain't Captain America," said a strangely pitched voice. "Back to suffer abuse or to hand it out again?"

I turned about. A heavy-set man with dirty blond hair tied up in a ponytail stood before me. He had on a thick fleecy coat that grazed his ankles, and wore a beaverskin hat studded with colored feathers. A pair of gold-rimmed glasses, with pink-tinted ovaloid lenses, sat at the end of his pitted nose.

"Yes, I like what I bought," I said, recognizing him as the joe who'd sold me my fur.

"Aye lad," he parried, "I grieve yet for that one." He

screwed up his face and held a fat hand to his forehead. "It came to me dear, and I sold it to you on the cheap ... But rob me again won't you please? Two wrongs will make it right, and the continents will be reunited."

He sputtered and spat at the ground. He smelt of whiskey.

"I want to buy some more."

"There, didn't I know it," he said. He removed a green silk handkerchief that he wore around his throat, and wiped the slobber carefully from his mouth. "When two Zen masters meet, they need no introduction ... thieves recognize each other instantly!"

He retied the scarf and grabbed me by the wrist. "Truth, lad. Do I not gabble justly? Come quickly if you wish to take me to the cleaners again."

His grip was iron. I tried to pull my arm away but it wouldn't budge. The day was slipping away; some of the less prosperous merchants were beginning to pack up their stands.

The man released me and I followed him to an area where rows of clothes hung from metal pipes. Two full-length mirrors were screwed into a makeshift wall of orange-stained veneer, with a black door set in between them. A girl of about fifteen, her back to us, was busy rear-ranging some ulster coats. Her head was wrapped in a rainbow-splashed bandanna; she wore a long dress flow-ered green and pink, and calfskin boots with hearts painted on them.

"Hi Veronica!" yelled my companion. "You're looking lovely as the May queen. If I had an ass like yours, love, I wouldn't find myself slaving for a miserable wretch like myself."

The girl turned to us. She had fair skin with straight blonde hair, cut at the neck. Her eyes were china blue and pregnant with adolescent wonder. Her nose was pierced with a gold hoop and several feathered earrings dangled from either ear.

The joe nudged me in the ribs. "Lovely lass, isn't she?"

His face twinkled in a rude smile; he half-covered his mouth with his hand. "Wouldn't I love to twirl its knickers about me ears," he hoarsely whispered.

"What ... are you saying about me ... Ralph?" said the girl in halting English. She pursed her lips, trying to look grave.

"I want to fly you to the moon, love, on my trustworthy rocket ship."

She blushed and opened wide her eyes. "What is stopping you?"

"Faith, Veronica," spluttered the man. "I'd sooner violate the amber neck of a bottle of ale, than plunder the consecrated ground of me hired help—and you of such tender age." He jostled me again with his elbow, a little too hard. "And several are the necks of ale bottles that would attest to that."

"I don't understand this," she said. She turned her back and took up the arm of a gray chesterfield hanging from the rack. She began flailing it vigorously with a stiff brush. "The police have been here," she said.

"What! The police?" Ralph reached behind his head and fixed the slip of orange ribbon that kept his hair in place. "What did the wanton alice bastards want this time?"

"I don't know," she said curtly. She continued striking the sleeve until it achieved a bright sheen.

"You needn't hold your tongue, Veronica. Not on account of this mate." He grabbed me around the neck with crushing fingers. "Why, he's nothing but another thieving merchant like ourselves—but twice as silent, and thrice shifty. Look at him, will you! Fitted up like a stable-mate of Satan, stinking of hashish and a king's harem-worth of nookie—rip out my tongue, if it ain't so!" He gave my head a good shaking. "No, you needn't hold out on us love. What did the vermin-ridden peelers want?" He looked from me to her, and let go.

"Please Ralph, it's not to talk about now." Her face reddened again; she kept her head turned from us.

"Ah—fine thing loyalty!" Ralph grabbed the girl around the waist, lifted her and planted a slushy wet kiss on her neck. She squirmed and tried pummeling at his head with her fists.

He let her go and stepped back. She feebly wiped at her cheek with the back of her hand. "You shouldn't do this, Ralph."

"Core—I shouldn't have been born, they should have drowned me like a kitten or a female of the Chinese race. It would have saved the world a moment or two of embarrassment ..."

He spun around and danced over to one of the mirrors. He primped the collar of his shirt and twirled the ends of his mustache. "Were they looking for stolen properties then, love—my God, I'm a meet ugly bastard!—ah no matter, it's all stolen anyway; say it's just and say it's so, Captain America, my dear. The poor steal from the rich and the rich take it right back. The former are jailed and the latter are praised, so need we dwell on ethics—I say screw the lot of them, rich and poor, animal and vegetable, father and son alike."

He led me around the corner, where four long racks of furs were hung in perpendicular rows, arranged by size and color. Evening's approach brought a drop of temperature; my ears were freezing, clouds of steam squirted forth from our mouths. The spirits of the dead animals howled silently in the winter twilight.

"It might be too dark to pick through them now," I said.

"We'll light a few lanterns. You can always review your purchases tomorrow. A small deposit will keep them from mischief."

Suddenly, a skinny boy wearing only a woolen shirt and a pair of corduroys came tearing out from around the bend, nearly knocking over a rack of furs. As he raced past us, Ralph stuck out a foot and tripped him; the boy went flying into a table of jewelry across the aisle. The vendors running the stand began shouting, and beating the boy with the backs of their hands.

In a stroke, they emptied his pockets, removing ten or fifteen watches and a slew of gaudy rings and brooches. The boy struggled to his feet. One of the vendors kicked him in the ass and he bounded off, nearly knocking over another few stands.

The men picked up the jewelry and packed it with their own wares. "Thank you, Ralph," said one. "I've seen that nitwit many times, looking at our things. He never took from us though."

"It's not surprising to me, lads," said Ralph. "Considering the ghastly crap you sell."

They laughed raucously and went about disassembling their stand. Ralph disappeared behind the racks and emerged with two lanterns. "Ho, mate, time is wasting." I rubbed my hands together and began looking through the furs as he rigged up the lanterns at the ends of two poles. Veronica appeared, lugging a box of sweaters.

I checked for unrepairable holes and signs of moths. If a coat might be good enough for further examination, I took it down off the rack and handed it to the girl. She stacked them on top of the box of sweaters.

"Do you have any with longer sleeves?"

"For men, what, you mean?"

"Yeah."

"They're passing rare. You're lucky to find one for yourself."

The coats were counterfeits, with authentic labels stolen from furriers in Paris and Oslo sewn into the collars. They were of good quality nonetheless. I brushed my hand along the entire surface of each piece, watching for where the fur might have thinned—no patchwork could fix that.

"Here, mate. Have a gander at this beauty."

"I have to look at each one myself. Try not to interrupt me."

Ralph stood in the aisle trying to squeeze a few last pennies from stragglers on their way out. "Come, come, my dearest ones ... I haven't made a sale all the friggin'

live-long day, I swear it by Mother's silver-hemmed wedding gown! Do you fancy that fair waistcoat? You needn't
try it on, you needn't pay me for it—just pull it down and
slip it quick into your sack... I only ask a small donation, a
pittance, sixty guilders—what too much? Make it fifty!—
the half of it to be given over to the Royal Society of Saint
Andrew of Malta, patron of the wretched and the impov-
erished, you must know of their mission in dark
Burma ..."

I picked out thirty coats. My eyes were beginning to
cross from concentrating, and still I had half a rack to sort
through. I held my numb fingertips to my temples, and
pushed my palm against my nose.

"Attention flagging, mate?" said Ralph approaching
me, licking his index finger as he counted a sheaf of bills.
He stuffed the currency into his pocket, cupped his hand
to his mouth and half-whispered in my ear: "Perhaps you
be in need of a pick-me-up, a freshener of the senses. Can
I ladle you up something from the devil's cauldron?"

Lantern in hand, he led the way down the nearly empty
aisles. Plastic sheets were thrown over the stands and tied
to the posts with rough cord. Dusk had slipped into dark.
We reached the primary entrance, where a pedestrian sky-
way rose from the grounds and crossed over a boulevard.

Beneath the iron stairway, a public lavatory was housed
in an aluminum-sided cabin. Two elderly female attendants sat behind a card table in a vestibule at the
entrance; the table was covered with a checkered cloth,
and held a narrow vase of flowers and a plate of coins.

Ralph clinked a guilder piece in the plate and
remarked something to the women in Dutch. They looked
puzzled.

"I said, you withered old crones," he shouted in
English, "to sound the gong should trouble rear its filthy
head!" For some reason, they began cackling, and we
passed through a door to the right, into the 'mens'. The
room was sparkling clean, with tiled floor and all chrome

stalls. Ralph produced a half-pint of schnapps and took a long drink. He wiped his mouth with the back of his hand and passed me the bottle.

"Ah," he said with devotion, "it's a right pleasing product, isn't it, my blood? Makes you want to get out and commit the sins of Noah ..."

I took a nip at the half-pint and passed it back. My toes and fingers regained some sensation, and my eyes loosened and began to uncross. The vapor of our breath hung in small clouds beneath the fluorescent bulbs in the ceiling. One of the faucets was dripping, and I could smell the wet brown paper overflowing the white bin aside it.

Ralph sat the bottle atop a ledge beneath a mirror. He snapped his hand at the wrist and slowly opened his fingers, producing a small vial on his palm. "Here you go, matey," he barked, tossing it to me. "See what you think. Light of the Andes and all that crap."

I unscrewed the top of the vial and caught the smell of alkali. White crystals nestled in powder glistened from within.

Suddenly, there was a frantic shouting from outside, and someone was banging on the tin siding. A louver was slit in the wall for ventilation; the distraught agitated voice of Ralph's assistant came through it.

"Quick," said Ralph, "it's the police come. Put that rig in your pocket. Haste, man." He turned on the faucet full force, removed his eyeglasses and set them down on the paper-towel container. He depressed the soap dispenser and a thin green liquid was emitted. He began to wash his face.

I stepped into one of the chrome stalls and lowered my pants. I sat down at the privy and fastened the latch. I heard the door open, followed by the thud of feet and the rattles of keys and chain. A crude atonal voice asked some questions. Ralph answered slowly, in Dutch, exceedingly nonchalant.

"Don't worry yourselves, officers," he said, switching languages. "We're but having a way-bit of schnapps and a good wash-up."

"Who is in there?"

"It's a mate, performing the rites of nature, sir."

Something scraped the floor. My ears began to burn and I had a strong sensation of unreality. I dropped the vial between my legs; the room seemed to darken. I looked up and saw the fleshy-jowled, waxen face of a white-hatted policeman glaring at me over the top of the stall.

"Do you speak English?"

"Yes."

"Come out, please."

"Okay." I reached behind my shoulder and pulled the chain. I slowly rose to my feet and pulled up my trousers. The policeman looked closely at the roiling waters.

The head disappeared. I undid the latch and walked out into the room. Ralph was gone. Another cop, younger, plainclothes, of higher rank, was standing against the wall with his hands in his pockets. He wore a pinstriped ash-gray suit, an Inverness cape and a thin, flowered tie over a pale plum shirt. His eyes were large and sunken, his nose finely chiseled; he had dark shiny hair, combed straight back.

I walked up to the basin and started to wash my hands. The fat-faced bull stepped up behind me. In the mirror, his hat seemed to be rising from my head.

"Please. Take off all your clothes."

I removed everything except for my undershorts and socks. He went through every pocket, turning each one inside out and dumping its contents on the floor. He pinched at the lining and the hems of my fur, and checked the cuffs of my jeans.

He took up my wallet and pitched it to the plainclothes, who meticulously counted my money, and proceeded to look at every scrap of paper inside.

I was extremely cold, for the bathroom had no heating. To avoid shivering, I held my breath, and kept my arms pinned tightly at my sides.

"Where are your drugs?" said the thick man in uniform. He had a long shaggy mustache that seemed to be growing out of his mouth; his face was otherwise utterly vapid, without meaning. I could hear his breathing now, he had a slight wheeze.

"I don't have any drugs."

He grumbled something to his superior. He stooped and stuck his fingers into my socks, scratching at my ankles in a lewd manner. He stood back up and kicked at my boots. Then he made me lean over and spread my asshole for him.

"Why are you in Holland?" he asked.

I pulled my shorts back up. "I'm on holiday."

"Where do you stay?"

I gave him the name of my lodging.

The younger man spoke up.

"Your name is Edward Verlaine?"

"That's right."

"Where is your passport?"

"In the safe at my hotel."

"You have a lot of cash money in your purse. Nine hundred dollars."

"It's not enough for me," I said.

His lips turned in a vague smile. He had a weary look, like he'd seen too much—I bit my tongue: it was queer to feel for a cop.

"How do you know this man from the market?" he asked.

"I don't know him."

"Shall we take you to jail?"

"I don't know him."

He reflected, looking at me with disdain. "Get dressed."

He instructed his adjutant to leave the room. The fat-headed man pulled at his bulbous nose. He picked up my fur and stared at me with scorn. He stepped on my T-shirt with a wet boot, and went for the door.

I pulled on my clothes. I picked up my effects and

stuffed them back into my pockets. The damp shirt stuck uncomfortably to my back. I blew on my hands to warm them.

"My name is Inspector van Velden, I am section head of the foreigner's police—specifically we investigate the crimes, and the criminal associations, of foreign nationals."

He looked me over with scathing eyes, well practiced at presuming and creating guilt. He spread his feet and leaned back against the wall. He clasped the fingers of his right hand over the left fist, and carefully massaged the knuckles.

"Mr Verlaine, the police have observed you in the company of known drug-traffickers—you have been seen frequenting their homes and meeting places. We find evidence of hashish in your pockets ... and we believe you have been using cocaine in this building before our arrival.

"These are serious criminal offenses."

He released his fist and pointed a finger at me. "As a foreign national, you have very few rights before the law. I can hold you in jail for three days without pressing charges. I can bring you before a magistrate, and he may remand you to jail for twenty-one days, without trial. We have no system of bail, and you have no right of appeal, nor may an attorney present any writ to free you. Do you understand?"

He removed my wallet from within his overcoat and extracted a small piece of paper from it. He held it up between his thumb and forefinger.

"This is the address of a flat on the Prinsengracht," he said calmly. "Why do you have it?"

"I don't know," I said. "I don't remember." All over my arms, the skin was hackled with goose bumps. A sickly smell of disinfectant trickled up my nostrils.

"The people who reside there are violent criminals."

"Well, let's go then," I said.

"What?"

"To the jail."

He looked at me with a detached glare, his eyes opening. "You don't want to tell me anything about these people."

"I don't know them."

"You don't know anything."

"No."

He locked his wrists together behind his back. He took a few steps across the room and stood facing the far wall. "We don't want you in our country, Mr Verlaine. You are trash." His voice echoed. I was careful not to move.

"You have disposed of the narcotics?"

I didn't say anything.

"Maybe you washed your dirty hands clean today," said van Velden. "That's okay—you will stick them in the shit again tomorrow." He turned around and walked up to me. The muscles around his eyes fluttered with a faint tic. "I would take little pleasure in locking you up for just a week, when I could have you for many years."

He put his thumb up to his mouth and bit off a piece of dead skin. One of his ears looked as if the lobe had been pierced at one time. He looked down at the floor.

"You know the girl named Jana, don't you?"

I didn't answer.

"What do you say?"

"A little bit."

His face turned steely, his mouth turned up in a sneer. He looked at me with deep contempt. "Wait here one minute."

He exited. I was shaking with cold and I felt that I was beginning to run a fever. I looked at myself in the mirror; my face seemed to be breaking out in splotches, but I didn't know if I should trust my eyes. Next to the mirror some graffiti was carefully drafted on the wall. One said: REAGAN SMELLS MURDER. Another read: HASHISH IS KING.

The fat man walked back into the room carrying my fur. He had an odd look on his waxen face, something in his eyes: the look of a ghoul. He walked around me and grabbed me by the hair. He yanked my head back as far as it would go without me falling over. Then he pulled me toward him until I heard the wheezing in my ear.

He released my fur and began punching me viciously in the kidneys, first one, then the other, still holding back my head. I balled my fists and bit down hard on my lip to keep from screaming. I kept my arms glued to my sides.

When he was finished, he dragged me over to the sink and turned on the hot water. With both hands, he pushed my face into the basin, and held it about an inch from the stream of the spigot. Scalding drops of water splattered on my nose.

After a minute, he let me go. He turned quickly and went out of the room. I sat down on the floor; it took me some time to regain my breath.

I splashed cold water on my face. I dried my hands and massaged my kidneys with my fingertips. I took a hard look at myself in the mirror; the dark image eluded me, breaking down into pores and veins cracking on the surface. The fluorescent lamps in the ceiling bathed the tile and enamel in a sharp, relentless light: everything was stark and empty.

I walked out into the market. It was dark and deserted; incandescent lights were strung on wire at its periphery. High above, the moon was nearly full. I picked my way through the aisles until I located Ralph's fur section. The long poles were empty, except for a few hangers that were soldered to the pipe.

I walked around the corner to where the coats and sweaters had been sold. I tried either door behind the stand, but they were locked tight. A flimsy folding chair was standing next to the wall. I picked it up and began smashing it against the full-length mirror.

No one came to stop me. I spat at the broken glass and threw the chair across the way. I repaired to the exit of the market and began walking back toward the center of the city.

I was on a boulevard. I saw the moon again dangling overhead, but its light held little value in the glare of the city. The town's personality was faded, in the drone and roar of trucks, in the starkness of concrete overheads, the bare traffic islands and the wide empty sidewalks. I was adrift in the industrial world: an endless sea of naked street lamps, of speeding metal, of polished rock and glass. I could barely breathe.

I headed over a wide canal and into the old town. The scenery softened, the buildings came closer together and I could feel the dull heat of mankind again, the glowing embers of flesh and spirit.

Soon I recognized the edge of the red-light district: long blocks of Chinese restaurants, brightly colored neon and backlit plastic signs affixed overhead. I walked haphazardly, crisscrossing the streets. I read the menus posted at the doors and studied the faces of the various clientele. I gawked at the rows of smoked ducks, hanging by their feet in the windows, beheaded and skinned.

I stopped in front of an outdoor automat; a bank of compartments was arranged in a rectangle, like safe-deposit boxes. The front of each compartment was glassed, allowing you to observe your meal selection. I dropped a guilder piece in the coin slot and took out a meatball on a paper raft.

Inside, behind the wall of the automat, a man served shish kebabs at a counter. Behind him, a yellow sign with purple letters broadcast the menu. I went in and begged a packet of duck sauce.

When I'd finished, I wiped my hands on a thin napkin. The main red-light area runs along two canals, the Voorburgwal and the Achterburgwal. The Achterburgwal is the ticket to ride, and I walked around, up a block and down a few, until suddenly, from out among the weaving streets, it emerged.

It was wide and spacious, oddly lit and mysterious. Every few hundred feet, a picture-book bridge spanned the two banks of the waterway, and men from all over the

world leaned against the stone railings. Sex shops, nightclubs, restaurants and strip-shows lined the banks. No
single establishment was especially interesting; they were
of a kind, except for a bar or two where they sold twenty-
five guilder packets of hashish in the basement, and
allowed you to smoke upstairs with a coffee or juice.

Running off the main street were many little lanes. At
their entrances you could look down and see short verti-
cal bars of red fluorescent tube jutting from the buildings.
Walking down the narrow passageways, you would pass
huge picture windows illuminated in pink and crimson
lights. A fake bedroom was put up in the window—sometimes a rather elaborate setting, with a beautiful sofa, oriental rugs and brocaded curtains. A woman would sit at a
chaise longue or settee, or perhaps be leaning against a
barstool, provocatively dressed in a flimsy silk smoking-
jacket, with bare legs and platform heels; or in a long
evening gown with the neckline plunging to the belly, face
made up like a sluttish princess, a glass of champagne in
her hand.

I stopped at one window. Inside, a woman of Eurasian
extraction, absolutely beautiful and perfectly formed, sat
at a burgundy armchair, hands folded in her lap, back
arched and legs spread. She wore a black velvet blouse,
unbuttoned down the length of her torso, revealing two-
thirds the orbit of her pale white substantial breasts. A
white silk skirt edged up past her thighs, showing the tops
of green garters clasped to diamond-patterned nylons.
Her look was hot and cold at once. She stared at me, her
eyes flaring, but was too proud to beckon.

I was gripped by a spasm of lust, something turned in
my stomach, and a wave of fear swept over me. I closed
my eyes and imagined what it would be like with her. I
pictured myself on my knees, unsnapping her garters,
unrolling her stockings inch by inch.

Desire overcame reluctance, and I opened my eyes
again, ready to pass through the windowpane and strike a
deal for her favors.

Her head was turned, and I saw that there was a man standing next to me, tall and well-dressed in a pale suit and speckled tie, a scarf wrapped smartly around his neck. He tapped at the window with his index finger. She signaled him and he went between the buildings and entered through a door in the alley while I watched through the glass. In a single motion she admitted him and pulled shut the curtain.

Crestfallen, I walked out the other end of the lane and joined the legions wandering aimlessly in the streets. I found a tavern filled with sailors and sat down at a stool. The bar was long and solid oak, a girl with orange hair and shaved eyebrows worked the spigots. The place was garishly lit, and the back of the liquor well was filled with idiotic sports mementoes: miniature soccer balls and cleated boots hung from the ceiling.

"*Wil je iets drinken?*"

"Dark beer."

One of the sailors shot his cookies on the bar. Two large men appeared. They grabbed him by the shoulders and rushed him out the front door. The barmaid cleaned it up in a matter of seconds and it was as if it had never happened.

After a while the sailors began to drift out of the bar. New people filtered in, younger, better dressed. The pitch of the noise shifted, yelling softening to droning, to near quiet. The lights dimmed. I could not get the desire out of my heart. I left too much money on the counter and went outside.

I walked around some more looking at the whores in the windows. The Eurasian was gone, her room deserted and dark. There were even more drunken people in the street now. Nothing clicked for me and I went into a different street, not as well lit, where the women stood against the walls and hissed, and were not so finely appareled. I did not respond to their calls, nor did I slow down.

The front door of the building on the Prinsengracht was

locked. I pushed the buzzer. No one answered. The night had grown cold, a wind was up from the sea.

I looked back at the canal; a hemisphere of pale orange lights shined from the arch beneath a bridge. A man and woman walked by, followed by a Pekingese on a leash. A police car drove slowly past.

On the third floor, the curtains of Margo Bellini's apartment were thrown wide open, and there was dull light inside. I picked up a handful of stones and threw them at the window. A few seconds later a key dropped down.

I climbed the flights; the stairwell smelled of perfumed floor wax and the steam of the radiators. The doorknob to the apartment gave in my hand.

The room was lit with a score of candles. They dotted the shelves of the bookcases and lined the windowsills. One window was cracked open and the smell of fresh air mixed with the scent of violets.

A woman sat at the couch with her back to me. A tall lamp with a tasseled shade stood next to her, illuminating a red satin bow affixed to her long dark hair. She did not react as I entered the room. I closed the door.

Her voice was slow and dreamy. "Who is that?"

"Eddie."

"Oh. Eddie. Yes ... I know. You are Jana's friend."

I walked across the carpet and approached the bay. I rested my palms on the sill and observed the bright face of Amsterdam: the geometric shapes where water met light, and sky married roof. The candles burning on the sill smelled of lemons, and there was an aroma of myrrh. No one said anything for a long while.

"Come and sit down next to me, Eddie. I was not so nice to you last time we met. Please."

I turned around and studied her face. In the lamplight her skin was uncommonly pallid, contrasting the rings of dark magenta and ultramarine that circled her eyes. I took a good gander at her long legs: they were hard to miss, stretching out forever from a scant plum skirt, a black widow spider tattooed inside the left thigh.

I seated myself, slowly sinking back in the cushions. I looked at her once more. Her hair seemed to be changing colors; it was hennaed with purple and sprinkled with glittering powders. A black hematite collar, painted with white stars and the planet Saturn, was clamped around her neck. Her breasts swelled beneath sheer lambswool.

On the table, next to a goose-neck lamp, Chinese joss sticks crossed each other in irregular grids. There was a pair of dice lying sixes up. A beveled mirror was mounted on a tarnished lion's paw stand: the glass was dense with spirals and figure-eights of white powder. Beside it lay a barber's straight razor, gold-handled and blade exposed.

Margo Bellini sat tranquilly, hands folded in her lap. "Eddie," she said, "I want to ask you something ... I can't figure it out." She tossed her head. A faint purple scar ran from beneath her ear descending toward the throat.

"I want to know—do you believe—is there more ... than what's in front of our eyes?"

"What do you mean?"

She flitted her lashes and formed her mouth in an o. "I keep seeing these things," she said, "a lot of things, strange and hard to know. For instance—do people carry auras? Do they throw off colors from their hearts?"

"Why not?" I said. "It's as likely as all the other shit."

"What shit?"

"I don't know. Electrons. The moons of Pluto. The gravitational pull of the Milky Way. All that crap they tell you about and claim as gospel, that you can't see, and never will."

She looked at me carefully. Her pupils were dilated; she slipped out the tip of her tongue, a dot of whitish pink filling in the raspberry o.

"Then what color are you?" she asked.

"Every color."

"You're not missing any?"

"Only one."

"Which one?"

"Sorry."

She tilted her head. A faint smile incubated upon her lips.

"What color am I?"

"Very hard to say."

She put her hand on my knee. On the middle finger she wore a wide silver ring engraved with alchemical symbols. She leaned her breasts towards me and I was enveloped with violets; it was hard work not to bite down on her lip and scream out the many names of God.

"Please say it," she demanded. "Tell me my color."

"You're the color that I'm missing," I said.

She pulled back her hand and shoved me brusquely at the shoulder. "You're good for parties, aren't you, Eddie? Why did you come here?"

"I don't know."

"To find Jana."

"I guess so."

"Are you disappointed?"

"Not yet."

She reached over the table. She stuck out her thumb— the nail was painted with an inverted cross, green on purple—and rolled a silver straw from beneath the lion's paw stand. She bent forward, touching her breasts to the table, fixated on the mirror. She raised the straw to her nose and inhaled a huge spiral.

She sat up, took a deep breath and exhaled. Her eyes gleamed with something risen from the dark, evil and delight. She made a sign with her finger, twice back and forth and once down, and proffered the straw.

I didn't move to oblige the offer. She opened her hand with a mincing gesture, releasing the object, and it fell to the carpet.

"Pick it up," she said. "You don't have good manners."

"Actually," I said, "I don't have any manners." I picked up the straw and tossed it onto the table; it clinked against an ashtray.

Margo folded her arms across her chest. She straightened her back and ran her tongue beneath the upper teeth. Her cheeks had reddened and her eyes were narrowed, barely showing white.

"Are you a smart man, Eddie?"

"I don't mind if you think that."

"What!" she said incredulously. "You don't mind?"

"No."

"Can you explain the world to me then?" She scratched her forehead with her long painted nails. "Do you know what everything means?"

"I hope not," I said. "That would be kind of sickening."

She crossed her legs and the fabric of her skirt pulled up over her thighs. A gust of wind entered the room, and the candles flickered.

"You don't think we are here together for a reason?" she proposed.

"No," I said. "It's just one stupid accident after another."

She sucked on the tip of her thumb. The wind whirled in again and the candle shadows flickered on her skin. My eardrums inflated and burned, as if I were traveling aboard a speeding elevator. She extracted the thumb, studied the saliva in the ragged light, and wiped it dry on her leg.

"Jana is far away," she said curtly. "Do you really miss her—or do you want your blessed money, the holy dollars?"

She got to her feet and walked to the kitchen with measured steps. "Excuse me for a minute." I heard her heels clicking on the linoleum, and then a door opened and was shut.

My eyes roved over the book spines in the bookcases. I withdrew a slim volume on Pintoricchio—Bernadino di Betti. There were reproductions of paintings that hung in Russia, that I'd never seen. The text was in Italian, but it was dry and technical, and I couldn't make it out too well.

I sat at the couch and studied the colors in the pictures. I tried some of the powder.

Soon I heard again the fillip of heels. Margo crept back

into the room and stood beneath a lamp in a dark corner.
Everything was still. Then she pulled the chain beneath
the funneled shade and she was showered in soft light.

She was dolled up in a scarlet camisole, fluted in black
and thin as tissue. There were white silk stockings that fitted above the knee, and stack-heeled paisley shoes with
straps that wrapped in helixes up her thighs. She'd
doused herself with more perfume, and my head reeled
with violets, the afterimages of Pintoricchio seared
behind my eyelids in shocking pink and blue.

I tried to collect my thoughts. "Where's your boyfriend
tonight?"

She arranged her hands on her hips and pushed out
her bottom lip. "Werner, you mean?"

"Yeah, that one. The killer."

"He's not my boyfriend. You are mistaken."

I stared out the window above the bay. The moon, a fat
white ball, was hanging low over the buildings across the
canal. I was filled with adrenalin, and the false powers of
the drug, and my imagination began to hemorrhage,
bleeding out into the room.

"Well—uh—do you have an understanding?"

"What are you talking about, Eddie?" she hissed. "Do
you think a man can own my mind?"

I shrugged my shoulders. "How about the rest of you?"

"The rest of me?" she said perplexedly.

"Besides your mind."

"The rest of me!" she exclaimed. "Really, sir! My body is
for my own pleasure."

She walked across the room out of my line of sight and
I felt her coming up behind me. There were strange shadows moving on the table, and I was frightened and exhila-
rated, my lungs bursting with her perfume.

She touched her lips to my ear. I thought of death, a red
coach heading for a dark mountain. "Don't worry," she
whispered. "Werner is gone far away on his business. You
are right to be afraid of him, but he will not return for
many days."

"What kind of business?"

She placed her nails on my throat, and clutched the cartilage of my ear between her teeth. "Is it me you are afraid of, Eddie?"

"I don't know," I said. "What should I do?"

"Drink some champagne while I unfasten your belt."

I did as I was told.

Afterwards we went into her bedroom. We lay on the sheets, propped on pillows, drinking brandy from a china teacup and smoking cigarillos of blond tobacco and hashish. A pair of speakers was bridled to the ceiling, and we listened to *Sketches of Spain*.

"Where do you live, Eddie?"

"London. Behind London Bridge."

"You don't get lonely for America."

"No."

She set the teacup on a night-stand next to a thick book with a red leather cover. She rested on her elbow and brushed her nose against my shoulder.

"Do you have a girlfriend?"

"I have a wife. Does that qualify?"

She took the skin of my deltoid in her teeth. "Does she care if you fuck me?" she said, biting down.

"No."

She released me. My skin was ringed with white alveoli. She grabbed my johnson with her long fingers, and began speaking at it in a contrived voice, as if it was a microphone:

"Attention! Eddie! Your wife is never jealous."

Her breasts were crushed over my ribs and the heat of desire began to waft up again. I leaned over and picked up the teacup, checking the marks on the bottom. It was a fine French name, and might fetch fifty pounds on the Portobello Road.

"My wife? What does she care?" I took a sip of the brandy; it exploded in my throat and eddied down, turning sweet.

"Do you love her?"

"I don't know. I love everything."

She unhanded me and motioned for the teacup. "Yes, Eddie, you are perfect for parties. Your wife loses nothing by keeping you." She rolled her tongue in the brandy. "Does she?"

"I guess you see it then."

"Is she an artist?"

"Yeah. She's an actress."

"What's her name?"

"Claudia Lansdale."

Margo's face registered surprise. She scrutinized me with wide eyes. "Claudia Lansdale? Really? I know of her. She has done something with Vittorini. *Under the Blade* it is called in Italian."

"That's right." There were no windows in the room, and time had lost its footing, burning up behind me like a fuse. "Are you a connoisseur?"

"Oh yes," she replied merrily, "I see everything. I love films—and books—all the foods for the mind."

She pulled out a thin drawer from the night-stand and withdrew a saltshaker of deep green glass. Ceremoniously, she unscrewed the nickel top. She dipped the nail of her ring finger into the neck and scooped up a tiny cone of white crystals.

Her eyes narrowed: "I love this too ...I love for my heart to beat fast, to speed up life—to run like an antelope on the long grass."

She forced it up her nose and set the vial down on the book. "What do you love, Eddie? Tell me truly."

I looked at her paisley shoes, which she had not removed. The straps had come undone and were hanging over the side of the bed. "I don't know," I said. "The Master of Flanders ... Antonello da Messina ... Jan Steen ... Lucas van Leyden ..."

"Painters from the old days. Yes, they're good ... But that's not enough." She shook her head, and her hair bounced on her shoulders, leaving a trail of glitter.

"There's no love in the second dimension. Emotion does not breathe in the flat world. Don't you love me?"

"Not at all. I don't think so."

She pouted her lips. "Do you love Jana?"

"I don't know."

She picked up my hand and bit it. She studied the ring of toothmarks, and bit it again. "Please do me once more." She shut her eyes tightly. "I want to make Jana very jealous."

I fell asleep. I dreamed that I was at a party with William Burroughs and Frederick Chopin. There were lots of girls there too, but they kept disappearing through a door. Chopin was pasty-faced, with pigtail, and dressed in a long velvet doublet. He was lost in thought and spoke to no one, finally disappearing himself, leaving me alone with Burroughs. We started talking about Friedrich Engels's factory in England, and something about autumn crops, and then someone was shaking me and I saw Margo, blurred, wearing a housecoat, very distraught.

"Quick, quick, quick, Eddie," she said. "Werner is home early—he is on his way up! You must fly."

I rubbed my eyes. It didn't make sense. My dream was too exotic to wake up in a state of terror.

"Does he carry a gun?"

"What are you saying? Hurry."

Someone had neatly folded my clothes over a dark oak chair. I slid out of bed and quickly put on my pants and shirt. "Where's my wallet?" I clapped my palms with frustration. "Tell me. Does he carry a gun?"

Margo skipped over to the bureau. An oval mirror was mounted on it, and it was covered with lovely little bric-a-brac. She opened the top drawer and took out my wallet. "We don't use guns here, Eddie," she said, pausing for a moment. "We kill with words."

I pulled on my shoes and put on my fur. Margo pushed the wallet into my pocket.

"I need my glasses."

"Glasses?" She looked perplexed and bit on a knuckle.

"You know—*occhiali,*" the Italian word popping into my head for some reason.

"Your eyeglasses are here by the bed. How do you know this word?"

Her housecoat was printed with bright flowers, orange and green on a field of blue. It came open as she reached down for the lenses. She let me look for a second, then pulled it closed with one hand, and placed the spectacles over my head with the other. She seemed to grow very calm. The glasses slid down onto the bridge of my nose, and everything came into clear dark focus.

The knob turned, and the door to the bedroom slowly opened. Werner walked in, his long carriage held straight and haughty looking. The great bear coat was draped over his shoulders, and an expensive leather bag was slung from his arm.

"*Scheiss,*" he said, looking down his nose at me. "You again." He turned to Margo. She had managed to tie the belt on her housecoat, and stood now impassively, her arms hanging loosely at her sides. She was barefooted and the make-up was wiped from her face. He said something to her in a dialect of German.

"You fucking pig!" she screamed. She turned heel and walked out of the room, slamming shut the door.

"You understand?"

"No."

Werner rubbed his hands together and blew on them. "A cold evening ... good to come indoors. What I asked her was whether she was screwing you—or robbing you." He threw the leather bag onto the bed and hung his coat on a peg next to the bureau.

I remembered Chopin and Burroughs and all the girls disappearing through the wall. Chopin, Chopin I thought, recalling his powdered face and waxen hands. I remembered the wind knocking off someone's hat at my sister's funeral. It rolled across the lawn like a hoop.

"I want my money back," I said.

"Your money?" His voice was thick with disbelief. He sneered and began to look through the pockets of his coat. "What money is that?"

"The money I gave you last night."

He looked over his shoulder and scowled down at me, flashing menace. "You must collect that money from Jana. It is not my responsibility."

I scowled back at him, my heart pounding. He turned and continued running his fingers through the pockets, looking for something, or killing time, stalling, to make me nervous.

Something flashed in his hand. It was the gold-plated straight razor from the sitting-room table. Werner flicked his wrist and the blade jumped from its housing. He held it high in the air, catching a dull gleam from the bulb overhead.

"This is a tool of the first-rate," he said. "I am a sportsman, you know. I have used it to cut the bellies from many fish."

I saw that the bed covers were thrown back, and the sheets mussed. I couldn't remember how the linens had been made when Margo and I first entered the room.

"Where did you get it?" I asked.

"The knife—in Italy of course." He blinked and rotated the blade a quarter turn.

"You like Italian goods."

"Don't we all." He looked at me strangely. "Yes — it is a nice country." He scudded the blade over the fat of his palm. "Communists, fascists and Mafia live together in harmony—no one pays the taxes, and the food is very good. And despite their reputation, they are quite honest people. They are too emotional to lie very well."

"Except for Margo."

He looked at me closely, with just a hint of amazement. Then he laughed—a high-pitched sound. With another flick of his arm he closed the blade and threw the razor on the bed.

He took a step forward and rested a hand heavily on my shoulder. "Listen," he licked his lips, his eyes shining, "I don't exactly understand you—but that's all right ...I am not afraid of what I don't understand."

A big white candle was burning on the nightstand. The wick was faulty, and a wisp of grey smoke came up into the air. "But I think you should not come here anymore," he continued. He exerted more weight on my shoulder. "Afterwards, each time, it puts us, the both, in a bad mood."

I nodded. The teacup, half-filled with brandy was sitting by the candle. I stepped over and picked it up. I smelled the liquid.

"You don't mind?"

He did not answer. I drained the cup and replaced it. "How do I find Jana?"

"Why?" The corner of his mouth twitched. He sat down on the bed and began to pull off his boots.

"What do you care?"

He twisted his face in contempt. "You don't find Jana," he said. He threw a boot across the room.

"Why not?"

He looked up and smiled. His upper teeth had been straightened and a diamond was set in the left cuspid. He pulled back his lower lip, baring the gum. The bottom teeth were crooked and disfigured.

"I said you don't find her. She finds you."

I went to the Leidsestraat and boarded a tram to the Rokin. I sat down next to a fat woman with a cocker spaniel on her lap. The spaniel wore a bright green and red sweater with little tin bells sewn on it.

I walked down a few blocks of cobbled side-streets. It was well past midnight, cold and tranquil. The passage-way was narrow and sparely lit; the people of the night drifted by with their heads bowed, speaking in hushed tones, their hands stuck deep in their pockets.

Three huge motorcycles were parked at the door of the

Bar Europa. They were well-kept and polished, the chrome gleaming. The handlebars had been custom-chopped, bent and turned upside down like devils' ears.

Inside, the immense hall was thick with smoke; the air was piqued by the bittersweet smell of hashish. The long rows of darkly-lit tables were lined with people and there was a ceaseless drone of drunken conversation. As I approached the bar I was caught in the whirl, a hundred candle-lit faces passing me, the endless tables seeming to revolve in opposing directions.

There was one seat left at the bar. I squeezed my way in and drank cognac and coffee for three-quarters of an hour. I thought about all the things that had flowed in and out of me, how they had been beaten and bleached of their meaning and returned to dust.

A new bartender came on. I recognized him from the other night. He wore a green shirt now, with a black bow tie; his apron was snow white and starched, rigid as cardboard. He serviced my empty glass, but he did not acknowledge me. He pointedly glanced my way several times, then turned his gaze when I looked up at him.

Presently he walked over opposite where I sat and carefully rolled up his sleeves two turns towards the elbow. He thrust his hands into the stainless steel basin beneath the counter, raised two soapy glasses and worked them over the scrub brushes.

"I see your friend is here tonight," he said.

"Who's that?"

He quickly immersed the glasses in the next basin, filled with steaming rinse water, and set them to dry on a clean striped towel. He pointed his chin in the direction of my left shoulder.

"You know, the leather girl. Jana. She was asking for you."

"Where is she?"

Someone down the bar called for a beer. The bartender stooped and removed a glass from the freezer; it was glazed with ice. He placed it beneath the spigot.

"She is sitting in the corner, with the motorcycle people."

I spotted Jana at a far end of the room, she was with three men dressed in elaborate black leather suits. They wore steel-studded chokers around their necks, and their hair was teased to stand up half a foot in the air.

Jana was seated on one of the men's knees, in a way so that she did not face me. She had a white bandanna wrapped around her head and wore huge hoop earrings. She had one hand about the fellow's neck and held a bottle of beer in the other. The group appeared somber, first talking in quick, animated spasms, then sitting mute and forgetful. One of the men had passed out, and his head was cocked back over the crest of his chair, his mouth wide open, his arms hanging limp at his sides.

I went and put two guilder pieces in the jukebox, and pushed some buttons. Someone shook me. I looked around. It was one of the men from Jana's table. He appeared to be about twenty-five, his face was unshaven and his eyes were cracked with red lines. He was on the tall side and stood with shoulders back, hands on his hips, with one leg set slightly forward.

"Hey," he said, in a pleasant voice. "Come on."

"What?"

"Come to our table, brother. Jana likes to see you."

I followed him to the table. I watched his arms swinging; his fingers were very long, with fingernails painted alternately orange and black. He wore silver rings on his thumbs, a thick set of keys was hooked to his belt.

There was an empty seat next to the man passed out. Jana and her paramour were seated opposite, the man who had guided me sat next to them. Jana put an elbow on the table and stared at me. Her face was heavily powdered and her cheeks rouged. She had shaved her eyebrows off completely and had painted on black and yellow bolts of lightning in their place. Her silver hair flowed out from under the bandanna, and strands of it were tied in thin braids and fastened with ribbons. Like the men, she was dressed all in black leather, and she wore a big crucifix around her neck.

"Eddie, hello again," she said softly. "I am glad to see you. I am thinking of you all day ... This is Dieter and Willem—and you know me." She put her hand against her breast. "I am Jana of the dark."

The man with Jana on his lap picked up a blue and white plastic pouch and spilled some black tobacco onto a cigarette paper. He was an odd-looking sort, his face long and dark, his eyes red as apples. His jacket was spangled with large silver stars and the shoulders were padded and hung with purple fringe. He raised a piece of red hashish from a foil packet, crumpled it between his fingers and sprinkled the crumbs over the tobacco. Nimbly he rolled the paper into a smooth cigarette, licked the gum and sealed it with his thumbs.

He picked up a silver cigarette lighter from the table and rolled the wheel, but it wouldn't spark. He looked at it incredulously and tried it again, without luck. "Royal fucking piece of shit," he said. "They stole from me a hundred pounds for it. I need a light. Jana—*heb je een vuurtje?*"

"Only between her legs," said the man with the painted fingernails.

Jana reared back her hand and slugged the fellow sharply in the mouth. He bared his teeth and there was blood running from the corner of his lips. He wiped it with his hand, looked at the red smear and began laughing.

"*Doet dat pijn?*" she asked.

"Yeah, yeah, it hurts," he said in English.

"That's nice. Pain is good for you, Dieter. It is like vitamins." She raised a finger and pointed at the man passed out next to me. "That is Oswald, Eddie. His brother has died these days. He is not taking it well."

"What did he die of?"

"He was hit by lightning." said Willem. He fumbled in Jana's pockets and found some wooden matches. He took one and slid his thumbnail across the tip, igniting it, and lit the cigarette.

"In the Netherlands?" I asked.

"No," said Jana. "In the Tanzania—on Lake Victoria. He was on holiday."

"It's an honorable death," I said. "Lightning in Africa."

"It's too hot," said Jana, as if she did not hear me. She unzipped her jacket; underneath she was wearing a low-cut white bodice, trimmed on top with royal blue silk. She cupped her hands over her mouth. "Oswald," she shouted. " Oswald! Wake up now."

Oswald remained in a stupor, neck crooked back over the rim of the chair, his eyes three-quarters shut. Jana reached over and shook him by the shoulder. He snorted and opened his eyes.

"*Ja*," he said meekly, sitting up. He was a slight person, with pale blue eyes and a fine nose. He had orange streaks painted in his hair.

"He died with honor," said Jana cynically. "Eddie says your brother died with honor."

Oswald pressed his forehead to his palms and shook his head back and forth. "*Nee, nee*, Jana." He clenched his teeth and grimaced. "Death is only black."

"You hear this, Eddie. Death is not honor." She rolled her eyeballs left and right. "It is not peace of mind... it is not floating in the sea. It is nothing ... nothing."

Dieter slammed his fist against the table, clattering the beer bottles. "No, Jana," he spit out. "You are wrong. Death is not the opposite of life—it is less than that, less than nothing." He ran both his hands through his spiked hair; it sprung back into place. "It is less than nothing."

Jana's man laid his cigarette in a tin plate and skimmed the ash with a matchstick. He seemed uninterested in the conversation. Jana wrapped her arms around him, and adjusted herself in his lap. "So, Willem," she said softly. "What do you say. Do you have an answer?"

He cleared his throat and freed his arms from her grasp. "You fools, don't you see?" He looked supercil-

iously around the table. "I say—and mark my words—
that drugs and liquor can conquer death." He picked up
his cigarette, took a draw and blew a thick cloud of smoke
out through his nostrils. "By imitating death, they defeat
death. They do it better than sleep ... We dream when we
sleep, don't we? Not like in death—which is dreamless.
But enough drugs and alcohol—we do not dream. And
yet we wake up alive."

Jana turned from him and looked out on the crowd.
"This is stupid talking, Willem. Tricks of the words." No
one spoke. Jana rested her head on his shoulder. "What is
sex then, Willem ...? Is sex like death? Tell me that is so. I
want to hear that." She rested her hand on his knee.

"No, no, Jana," he retorted. "Sex is a trick. A magic
trick. It tricks you into thinking that life has meaning,
that death will not come."

Jana sat up and leaned over the table. I picked up the
cigarette from the ashtray; it still carried a spark. I took a
draw and then exhaled; stars danced across the table.

"What do you say now, Eddie?" asked Jana. I felt her
toe nudging my leg under the table. "How do we explain
it?"

"It doesn't mean anything. Not life, not death."

"What if my death comes tonight, Eddie? It won't mean
anything?"

"No."

Oswald began sobbing. He pressed his cheek to the
table and cupped a hand over his ear. "My brother is
gone," he said. He wiped his fingers against his wet face.
"He did not finish his life."

Jana kept her toe against my leg. She whispered something into Willem's ear. The noise level of the room slowly
increased. Some people at the next table began speaking
in French. The lights were dimmed and candles were set
on the bar.

Jana and Willem got up. "We are going for a ride," he
said. "We shall return soon." He had unbuttoned his
jacket. A pair of copulating elephants was tattooed on his

hairless chest.

They walked off. Oswald blew his nose into his hand and wiped it on his pants.

I got up and followed them. There was a huge clot of people at the door. Everything was buzzing like a beehive about to be set on fire. I shouldered my way through. A woman with sunken eyes and large breasts smiled at me, but I could not stop.

Outside the side-street was nearly deserted. The moon was touching the tip of a distant gable, like a coin balanced on a triangle; the air was bitterly cold. Willem was jumping on the kick start of his bike. He couldn't quite get it to turn over.

Jana stood against the wall of the building, looking up at the sky. I walked up to her.

"The moon is the god of death," she said without looking at me. Her eyes seemed glazed and her voice was flat.

"Don't change the subject," I said.

"What do you mean?"

"You owe me four hundred bucks—you can skip the bullshit."

A large Alsatian was tethered to a column next to the bikes. He started growling ferociously and straining at his leash. Willem yelled something in Dutch, but the dog did not heed him. He started pulling in my direction, growling and showing his mucous-coated teeth.

"Money," said Jana. "What is money compared to death, Eddie?" Some people passed by, dressed in silken robes and turbans. They turned into an alley and disappeared. The wind came up, blowing hard with frost.

I slapped Jana across the face. She did not react. I slapped her again.

Willem grabbed my arms and pulled them behind my back. Jana looked at me, her countenance losing definition, so that everything was her eyes, blank and extending back right through her skull.

"Why are you doing that, Eddie?" said Willem. The wind made his voice warble in my ear.

"Because I'm pissed off."

Jana held a hand to her cheek where I'd slapped her. The emotion returned to her and she crossed her arms and held them tightly against her chest. "It's okay now, Willem," she said. "He's from the land of violence. They shoot first their guns, then they talk. I owe him some money."

Willem let go of my arms. "How much?" he asked. Jana said nothing. She had begun to cry.

"How much, Eddie?" said Willem.

"Four hundred dollars."

"That's piss to fight about."

I nodded my head. The dog went into a frenzy. He seemed like he would break his leash. Willem went over to him and grabbed him by the jaws. He got on his knees and whispered in the dog's ear. Finally the animal calmed.

A light dusting of snow began to fall, and the flakes melted as they landed on our faces. The moon had begun to drop behind the building and the snow fashioned a veil of gauze in front of it. A large snowflake landed in my eye and Jana appeared to be melting against the wall.

Willem climbed back on his bike and kicked the starter. It turned over this time, filling the air with a powerful noise. He turned the handlebars, revving and desisting until the bike attained a smooth idle. Then he pulled back one of his sleeves and unfastened a wristwatch.

"Catch." He tossed the watch at me. I caught it in my right hand. It was heavy, and encrusted with jewels. A skull was painted on its face and the hands were bones.

"The watch is worth ten-thousand guilders. They say it belonged to Aleister Crowley." He shouted over the noise of the engine: "You shall keep it as security until Jana repays you."

"Okay." I put it in my pocket.

Jana approached me. She embraced me and spoke quietly. "Don't be mad at me, Eddie," she said, in a little girl's voice. "I will make it up to you tomorrow." She held me tighter. I put my arms around her waist, I couldn't control it, nor did I want to. The smell of exhaust from the bike mixed with her smells and the damp musk of my fur.

"Come, Jana."

The next day I returned to the flea market at noon. The sun was out, and it was some sort of office holiday. There were a good many people milling about.

There was a stand that carried old postcards and faded prints torn from books. I flipped through several boxes of the cards, looking at the stamps and watermarks. A few looked inviting; I put them in a pile on the table.

I looked through the prints, one by one. I found a couple of hand-colored maps of the British Isles that might be tricked-up with a frame, and profitably sold in London. I paid for my purchases.

Ralph paced back and forth in front of his stand. He held a cigar butt in his hand and was talking to himself. When he saw me, he tossed aside the stogie, rushed up and grabbed my hand with both of his, and began pumping it up and down.

"Mate! Mate! Bless all the fates—the bulls have left you untouched. You had me right worried and seeming frightened. I thought they'd surely have tossed you in the clink, or put you on the first flight back to Yankee Stadium." He released my hand and began to adjust my collar.

"It doesn't matter," I said. "Do you have my furs?"

"What is it, lad?" He turned his palms up in the air. "You're not carrying a grudge are you? Say it isn't so ... I didn't know the peelers were fast upon us. I lost me a good thousand guilders worth of blow in the bargain. You did some frightening job of palming the stuff. Where in the name of Christ did you stick it?"

"You mean they didn't give it back to you?"

Ralph blinked a few times. He scratched at his face; he was sorely in need of a shave. "Eh—what do you mean, mate. I don't follow."

"Do you have my furs?"

Ralph clasped his hands together and stood thoughtfully for a moment. One of the templepieces of his spectacles had broken off, and the lenses sat crookedly on his nose. His left eye twitched.

He unclasped his hands and indicated with his right index finger. I followed him along the racks of clothes. The air was crisp and cold, and the smoke and vapor of people's breaths mixed with the winter sunlight.

We rounded the corner and approached the two doors in the orange wall. The broken mirror had been covered with a sheet of plastic. Ralph opened one of the doors and led me inside.

The room was small, ill-lit and crowded with boxes. His assistant was sitting at a makeshift desk. Her hair was pulled up on top of her head and dotted with flowers; a pair of pagodas swung from wires in her ears. She smiled at me.

"Where's Captain America's box of furs, Veronica, love? He thinks I blowed him out to the bulls—imagine!"

She didn't reply. She got off her chair, stooped down and looked through some boxes beneath the table. Finally, with Ralph's assistance, she lugged one out.

"Here we go, mate! Such as you chose them. We'd prayed for your return."

"Help me take them outside." There was an edge to all the proceedings now. But things couldn't be rushed.

The girl pulled the box outside. Ralph looked on disdainfully. I kneeled on the ground and took out the furs one at a time, spreading them on the asphalt.

"Watch it mate! You'll get them mussed."

Some of the pelts had been switched for inferior ones. I put them in a separate pile.

Ralph crouched down and put his hand on the fur I was examining, clamping it to the ground. "Hey, now, what's the gig, mate? This is a package deal, you know. Used merchandise. This ain't fuckin' Harrods."

I looked up at the girl. "We have many nice furs," she said to me averting my glance. "Don't worry, Ralph." She touched him meekly on the shoulder. "It will be okay."

Ralph got up and shook his head. "These bastards think they're king of all shit, don't they. All right. I'll be in the office." He turned and passed through the door.

I continued my examination. The girl watched wistfully, her hands behind her back. "Your mind is not like you look," she said. I picked up my head. Nervously, she smoothed down the front of her shirt.

"Call your boss."

She went into the storeroom and closed the door behind her. After some minutes, Ralph followed her out; his face had a warm glow to it. The girl's eyes had reddened and her stare was vacant. I ruffled my hair with my hand.

"There's seventeen furs here that I want," I said. "They're far from perfect. I'll give you five hundred guilders for the lot."

"The fuck!" screamed Ralph. "You're off your bleeding bean, you wank!" His hands shaking with rage, he started putting the good furs back in the box. "This isn't the bloody cocksucking Sisters of Mercy charity shop, sir."

"And not Harrods."

"This is quality merchandise—top of the line," he spluttered, looking up at me. "You look around. You'll find nothing like this. Nothing."

"All right. Maybe I'll be back a little later." I turned and slowly began to walk down the lane.

"Wait a minute, lad," Ralph cried out. I kept walking. A woman in a wheelchair was looking at sieved spoons.

Ralph was next to me. I stood still. "Let's not be too hasty, lad." The brisk walk of ten yards had him nearly breathless. "I admit," he panted, "I'm in sore need of some coin ... Perhaps I could adjust a bit."

"Okay."

"Eight hundred guilders."

"That's forty-seven a head. The first one I bought cost me fifty. That's six percent discount for buying seventeen. Make it six hundred."

Ralph grabbed my sleeve with one hand and put the

other arm around my neck. He stank of whiskey. "Come on now, mate," he said gibingly. "What's your real game? ... Why are we fighting about a hundred guilders?"

We had stopped in front of a stall that sold decks of cards and pairs of dice. There was a sign at the table with a medieval joker pasted in the middle of it. I shook myself loose of Ralph's grip and picked up one of the decks.

The cards had exquisite little flowers for pips. I thumbed through until I found a picture card. It was the king of hearts. He was wearing a long green robe with red piping, and impaling himself with a dagger.

"Can you deliver the merchandise to my hotel?"

"Yes, sure."

"Seven hundred."

"Half up front—add twenty for delivery."

I went to the Van Gogh Museum to look at the paintings. I don't really give much of a hoot for him, but I guess he's better than most of the Impressionists. That gang didn't seem to have much focus, and not a drop of emotion.

Van Gogh did paint a few nice ones right before he committed suicide. So I went to look at those. Here he was into it. With death sitting on his shoulder, he got behind the scenes and transcended. Monet attempted suicide several times—his first wife died of malnutrition—but you wouldn't know it to look at those lily ponds and haystacks. Form divorced from feeling. But Van Gogh's bad luck was our good luck. Funny how it works.

In a special anteroom I spotted several of Van Gogh's copies of Japanese woodblocks of the seventeenth century. They were precise imitations, and would have fooled Hiroshige himself. The master artist as master thief.

I went to the gift shop. Sometimes it was easier to look at the postcards than the paintings. There were lots of prints and cheap posters as well, awful to behold—Van Gogh's insanity does not reproduce well. I picked out a few cards for my collection.

I pulled out my wallet as I went to the desk to pay.

Between some twenty-guilder notes in the billfold I found a mauve business card with green lettering. The typesetting was in an art deco font, and said:

FROZEN ALICE. VINTAGE CLOTHING, ANTIQUES, ODDITIES.

On the obverse was a hand-written note in blue fountain pen: "This is my shop. Please come for a visit. Margo Bellini."

I took a tram to the Spui. I stood upstairs in the big magazine store and read an obscure Canadian fiction journal. There was a story about some existentialists robbing a drugstore in Quebec City; a woman got shot in the heart by a security guard and a pink haze rose off her body. I leafed through an oversized Italian fashion tabloid and watched a girl in white glasses shoplifting a map.

Out in the square, men in suits and ties were crowding into one of the pubs for lunch. A swarm of smartly dressed students whizzed by on their ancient bicycles. The air was crisp and clear and I felt that I had awakened into a dream and that I wanted to live forever in this single moment. My sister was dead, buried with all the billions who had lived before us, but for some reason I was still here. It didn't seem possible.

I turned into the Huidenstraat, where Margo's shop was located. I walked along the sidewalk of the narrow street, peering into the show windows of the avant-garde boutiques. I passed a store with a six-foot toothbrush in the window, and another filled with busts of Elvis Presley. I looked through the smoked glass of a tiny bar. A man in a white suit and a top hat was sitting at the counter, a long cigarette holder braced between two fingers.

The window of Frozen Alice was filled with mannequins. They were all dressed in red lingerie, and wore earrings and high-heeled shoes. A black table hovered above them, suspended from the ceiling.

I walked inside; the door was heavy and rung some tinny-sounding bells. The room was filled with racks of vintage clothing, the floor was crisscrossed with faded oriental carpets.

Margo was standing next to a burled chest of drawers talking on a green telephone. She was dressed in a white satin blouse and a rose silk skirt, with a black scarf wrapped around her throat. She wore a purple pillbox hat, with a pearl brooch affixed to the brim, and purple shoes, open-toed with silver buckles. If looks could kill, they would have had to call me a priest.

She waved at me. I sat down on a red love seat and rested my feet on a low table. There was a Persian tea service laid out; a deck of Thoth tarot cards was spread in a fan. Margo's back was turned to me and I watched her rear end for awhile, marveling at the black seam that ran down the back of her nylons.

"No, no, you don't understand," she said into the phone. "That's not enough time. That's not enough money. It's not enough of anything." She started shouting in German and hammered the receiver against the wall. She listened again, said nothing, and finally slammed the receiver down on its cradle.

"Shit!" she said, walking towards me, wildly waving her hands. "That fucking bastard. I am going to kill him. Do you know what happens when my blood is boiling? Whoosh!"

She sat down next to me and put her arms around my neck. I was enveloped in a cloud of violets and my heart rate jumped fifty beats. Still, I had the presence of mind to stick my nose into her bosom, and hold it there complacently, until she released me.

"Come, Eddie—let me look at you." She pushed me back with her hands. "I don't know why, but I am glad to see you. You are always the same, aren't you?" She tapped me on the cheek with her fingertips and tweaked my nose.

She stood up and climbed on my lap, kneeling, and began kissing me all over the neck and ears. I stuck my hand over her rump and pulled her against me. She had on long silver earrings that whipped against my face; she stuck her arm under my shirt and dug her nails into my skin.

I tried to guide the action but she would have none of it. So I just sat there and took it like a man. Then I was on my back and she started shaking me by the shoulders and screaming in Italian and French. My view was filled with satin, silk, and flesh, and then I closed my eyes and I went up to the sixteenth level of desire and stayed there for days and days and then I was gone and I just heard the screaming, and then it was calm.

We sat at the table drinking tea and eating chocolates. Margo flicked open a silver compact; the underside of the lid was mirrored and reflected a brimming concave basin. She serviced each nostril with a tiny shovel made of jade.

She tendered the box to me. I sampled a trifling dose.

Margo looked at me through slitted eyes. "Will there be anything else for you, Eddie?" she said coolly, buttoning up her blouse. "I have to go back to work, you see. The wolf is at the door."

"What do you have to do?"

"Well, everything, you know. The buying, the selling, the bookkeeping. And then, when that's all done, I take my dreams and splash them all over the sidewalk ..." She pulled her hair back in a ponytail and began rigging it with pins and combs. "Is that all right with you, sir?"

"I don't understand," I said. "About your dreams."

"It is what we do," she replied. "When we are hungry, when we are old, when we lose our art. We don't tell our dreams anymore—we sell them. We change what we see in our minds to everyday forms, and charge cash money."

She picked up the jade shovel and licked it off. "How do you live?" she asked. "Do you beg from the women you fuck? I don't think so. Your outside is soft enough, but inside is something hard."

"I work in the flea markets in London," I said. "Same basic action. Buy low, sell high and cheat ..."

She held out a diamanté mirror and began making herself up. She blurred some rouge across her cheeks, and dabbed her nose and throat with powders. "Are you taking anything home with you to sell?" she asked. She picked up a glitter pen and carefully painted a star on her forehead, and one on her chin.

My teeth were clenched with the drug. I poured a jigger of whiskey in my tea and took a drink. "I bought some old furs in the Waterlooplein. If I tart them up a little, I think I can triple my money."

She put the make-up down on the table and ran her palm over the tarot deck. She pulled a card and flipped it over. "Deuce of Wands again!" she exclaimed, disgustedly. "What's with this fucking card? It's following me like a ghost ... Who fixes up the merchandise for you, Eddie, to make it ready for resell?"

"I don't know," I said. "I've never tried pushing furs." I poured some more whiskey into my tea. "Do you have any idea?"

"Well, yes, of course—old clothes is my business." She flipped up another card. "Oh, what is this now!" she blurted. She shook her head and made some kissing sounds. "Queen of Cups—ah shit—I will have to cancel all my appointments ..."

"What's your idea?"

Margo looked up from the cards. She tugged on one of her earrings and screwed down her lips. I felt jittery; the room seemed to be tilting. I thought I heard the sputtering of a motor. A blue parakeet swooped from the ceiling and landed on a rack of zoot suits.

"I have a girl who comes to do this work. We have a machine in the back."

"I need it done by tomorrow."

"You're leaving us so soon, Eddie?" she said reproachfully. "Just when we are getting acquainted?"

I nodded. She brushed her fingertips over the cards. The parakeet circled the room in an oblate circle, clumsily beating its wings, and crashed into the wall.

"That bird is sick—but in the head. What is it Anna Christie?" she shouted. "Go back to your cage and take

your pills ... Okay—here's what we do, Eddie. The girl can
come in tonight after I close. You will pay her one and a
half times the wage, and twenty-five guilders to me, for
use of the shop. This is cheap."

"I'm broke," I said. "I can barely make the rail fare to
the Channel."

"No money?" She glared at me. "Nothing happens
without money, Eddie. The sun falls from the sky. Europe
sinks into the ocean."

"I'll wire you—"

"Wire?"

"I'm good for it."

"You're only good for one thing, Eddie." She chewed on
her thumb. She took up a pencil and scrawled some
hieroglyphic numbers on a notepad. "Is your wife really
Claudia Lansdale?"

"Yes."

"Where will you sell the furs?"

A blotch of apricot appeared in front of my eyes. I shut
tight the lids, and it disappeared into a funnel. "What do
you care?" I said. "It's not important."

"Fuck that, buddy," she retorted. She pressed the flat of
her palm against her forehead. "Everything is important
when I am talking to you. Especially if you want something from me."

"The Portobello Road, I guess. Depends how good they
look."

"If we do it, it will look like God's finger touched
them ..." She picked up the compact and shoveled some
more product up her nose. She dipped her fingers into the
teacup and dabbed the droplets beneath her nostrils.

"Yes—it will be the Miracle of the Rose ...who did you
buy the coats from?"

I looked at her wearily. "It's no big deal," I said.

"Oh no, oh no, oh no." She shook her head vigorously.
Her eyes opened wide, as if in terror. "Every little deal is a
big deal. That's the only thing I ever learned in life. The
hair that is out of place is the one they will use to kill you

with." She pulled at her fingernail and pumped her fist. "Who'd you buy them from?"

"You wouldn't know them."

"I know everyone in this business. Is it the man with the yellow eyes?"

"No."

"Then it's mad Ralph, of course. The false Englishman."

I didn't answer her. "Tell me more," she demanded. "Tell me."

I felt cold, and I tried to think of something clever, but I drew a blank.

"Nothing to say? That's all right." Margo stood up, leaning her weight against the wall for support. "Bring me what you want tonight at half-past five. We will take care of it ... Do me one favor, though—"

She took an unsteady step forward—she was beautiful and drunk. I reached out my arm and she grabbed it.

"You will keep your thing out of other girls today." She stuck her nails into my skin. "Do you hear me?"

"Okay."

When I returned to my hotel, Werner was waiting for me. He was leaning against the brick façade, one hand in a pocket. He was wearing the great white bear coat, unbuttoned, revealing a gray pinstriped suit. A small black tie was fastened tightly at his throat, overwhelmed by the collar of a fine silk shirt. He was smoking a cigarette with a gold filter tip—he flicked it dramatically with his thumb, sending a shower of sparks into the air.

A bright red and white metal sign, broadcasting the name of the hotel, was screwed into the brick next to his shoulder.

Seeing me, he ground the cigarette into the sign, leaving an unpleasant smudge, and tossed the butt onto the sidewalk. It landed a half foot from the curb.

"Not very Dutch of you, is it?"

He looked up, pretending to have just noticed me. "I

told you I am from Germany, Eddie," he said, rising to his full height from the wall. "We are clean by habit, not by instinct." Then, in a strange pristine manner, he took a small packet of paper tissues from his breast pocket and removed one. He dabbed the corner on the tip of his tongue, and carefully removed the smudge from the sign. Then he walked up to the curb, and with the side of his shoe, he pushed the cigarette butt into the gutter.

"There we are," he said proudly. "All neat and clean again—as it should be. First we destroy. Then we create. No one can stay angry for long—and besides, no one can remember what happened before."

I nodded. "It's an old country that you come from," I said.

"Yes, very old. All these countries. Our throats are filled with history." He walked back to the facade of the hotel and sat down on the stoop that accessed the lobby. He removed the thin gray gloves that he was wearing and laid them fastidiously in his lap. He rested his palms on the cement and appeared to be lost in thought. Someone came to the door and stared out at him, then retired.

Werner licked his lips and put another cigarette in his mouth. He let it hang from his teeth, unlit. "I do not like history," he said, without the cigarette moving, speaking from the throat. "History does not ever tell us when a man is speaking the truth, and when he is giving the lie."

A wind came up. I fastened the catch at the top of my fur. Across the street a woman was walking an Irish wolfhound. The dog tugged hard on the leash and nearly pulled her over. She caught her balance and grabbed on to her hat.

"Why are you putting your nose in my business, Eddie?"

"Which part of your business do you mean?"

Werner lit the cigarette with a thin black lighter. He inhaled deeply and blew the smoke out of his nose. The wind caught it and pushed it back around his face. "How many languages do you speak, Eddie?"

"Only one."

"I speak seven. And then one more ..."

"What do you mean?" My hands were freezing. I rubbed them together. The skin was cracked and dry. I looked down the street. In the distance I could see the lawns at the edge of the Museumplein.

"I speak seven languages," repeated Werner. "And then one more, the eighth—the language of violence." He opened his eyes up wide, and stared at me. "Three days ago I don't know you from anything. Now every time I turn my head, you are there."

"I don't mean any harm."

A man in a green coat walked out of the hotel. His face was shiny and his hair was swept back with pomade. He looked down at Werner and said in stilted English, "Please, sir. You will have to move. You are blocking our entrance."

Werner said nothing. The man stood his ground, looking down sternly at him. "You must move, sir. I can call you a taxi, if you wish."

Werner showed his upper teeth, shining white and straight, like those of an expensive dog. He focused on his lap, bowing his head, and in a low voice, began speaking in Dutch. He repeated something over and over.

A look of shock passed over the man's face, then he blushed deeply. He turned and walked back inside. The door closed soundlessly.

"The stupid asshole."

Werner's face grew passive again. He finished his cigarette and threw it in the street. He got to his feet and walked up to me. He smelled of cologne and tobacco. There were fine pink polka dots on his necktie.

"Why do you buy all these furs?"

"It's cold."

"To take them back to England?"

"Okay."

"As long as you are going to all the trouble ..." he paused and looked around, his features softened, "would you like to take something more profitable with you? It does not take up very much space."

"No thanks," I said. "I don't like to worry."

He sniffed at the air. His eyes changed color, the green became deeper, the whites turned to porcelain.

"You don't look like a worrier, Eddie."

"I trained myself," I said. "It's not by instinct. Are you finished with me?"

Three couples walked out of a gray stone building. The women wore tight-fitting mink coats and hats that glistened with oil. The men carried architecturally-designed cameras. They spoke in hushed, excited tones, and walked past without looking our way.

"Swiss bastards," said Werner, not too softly. "Worse than Americans. Think they own the fucking world."

"Are Germans so popular?"

"Yes, that's right, Eddie ... But we earned our reputation." The tourists crossed the street. One of the women stole a glance at us.

Werner turned to go. He looked back and pointed his finger at me. The street was deserted and all the buildings were perfectly made and the sky was washed with light blue.

"Don't forget, Eddie. *Arbeit macht frei.* `Work makes you free.' You know who said that?"

"Marx?"

"No. Hitler. Marx said that work will kill you. Beware, my friend." He stuck his hands in his pockets and began walking down the Jan Luykenstraat. A swarm of pigeons, gathered on the sidewalk, beat their wings and flew off as he approached them.

Werner disappeared around the corner. A small police car, the lights on top turning, pulled up to the curb. Inspector van Velden climbed out of the passenger's seat and strode quickly towards the door of the hotel. A very young, uniformed policeman came out on the driver's side and, keeping a careful eye on me, walked around the back of the car.

The man in the green coat stepped out of the hotel and grimly greeted van Velden. They talked for several minutes, the hotelier nodding my way every few sentences. He handed the inspector an envelope and retreated back inside.

Van Velden walked toward me. He had on a gray herringbone suit, a pink shirt and a pale green tie; a raincoat was dropped over his shoulders. He wore pointed Italian shoes that glistened with wax and spit, and the point of a handkerchief peeked out of his breast pocket. There was a vague sneer on his face and he looked ready to eat me for dinner.

I closed my eyes for a moment and tried to think of Bosch's circular portrait of *The Prodigal Son*, which I had seen a few days previous in the museum at Rotterdam. Instead of the excited family gathered round their long lost kin, one spotted, rather, in the left distance, a peasant pissing on the wall of a tattered barn.

Something poked me in the spine. "Come with me into the car, Verlaine. I want to talk to you. Step quickly."

We marched forward toward the auto. My throat filled with needles. The boy in uniform stood erectly at the curb, palms rested on his thighs. Van Velden opened the hind door of the car and I got in.

The door slammed shut. The interior smelled of plastic and coffee. I slid back in the seat. Outside, van Velden addressed the boy; his voice passed through the glass in a quavering tone, as if it were traveling through water.

A mesh grill separated the back seat from the front. A hinged plate, six inches by eight, was set in the middle of the grating. Van Velden climbed into the car. He turned about and stared at me with insouciance.

"You stink of hashish. Are you holding any shit?"

"No," I said. I had at least five grams in my boot.

He tapped on the window. His confederate opened the back door and got in next to me. He couldn't have been much older than eighteen; a slight wisp of beard cob-

webbed from his chin, and his face had erupted in acne at
the forehead and in the orbits beneath the eyes.

Van Velden gave him an order. The boy began to probe
my pockets with leaden fingers. He patted down my fur
and trousers.

"You are very pretty girl."

A microphone moored beneath the radio began to
squawk. The inspector picked it up and began talking into
it in a clipped fashion. The boy slapped me on the thigh.

"You know," he said slowly, "you are some garbage."

I smiled and took a good look at him. "Your mother is a
prostitute," I said.

His face reddened, and his ears twitched. "What do you
say!" He made a fist, ready to strike me.

I shrugged my shoulders. Van Velden cradled the
microphone. His subordinate began speaking angrily to
him.

"What did you say to my man?"

I didn't answer. Van Velden picked up a clipboard,
made a notation, and set it down. He looked at himself in
the rear view mirror. He pulled down at the skin beneath
the right eye and fluttered the lash. He said something to
the boy and hit a button on the console, unlocking the
back door.

The boy grunted and then pulled on one of my earrings. "You are pretty girl." He blew in my face; his breath
was faintly rancid. He climbed out of the car and crossed
the street. I could hear his heels clicking on the cobble-
stone. Van Velden twisted around and looked at me.

"What do you want?" I said.

He pushed his face up against the grill and grasped at it
with his hands. His nostrils flared. "I want you to stay
away from Jana," he said slowly. " I never want you to talk
to her again ... I never want you to think of her again."

"I thought she was working for you."

Van Velden pushed a hand to his jaw. One of his eyes
twittered. "You're ridiculous, Verlaine," he said sternly.
"Do not play the fool that you look like ... She is a friend of

my family—I have known her since we were little children."

He toyed with his cuff links; he moved his face so that it was obscured by the steel plate. "What do you think?" he said. "That a police officer should not be friends with a girl like that? That I would only wish to know women who stay at home and bake the cookies, and wash the kiddies' noses?"

"You're losing me."

"No, no," he said hurriedly. "You're already lost—a long time." He pointed his pinkie finger at me, and touched the thumb to his lips. "You're in the wrong place, Eddie—a very few inches from the edge of hell. You're mixed up with dangerous people. I told you that last time. You did not hear me."

From the seat, he picked up the envelope that the hotelier had handed him. He fished a Polaroid photo out of it and held it by the corner up against the grate. It was a shot of me and Werner sitting on the hotel stoop. It had been taken through the glass door and was covered with a strange glare.

"It is a bad idea to have your picture taken with Werner Brandt. If our side sees it—it could put you in jail for the long count. There is a nice place that Interpol uses in northern Africa, fully equipped with fire ants and brown scorpions."

He slipped the photo back into the envelope, slid his tongue over the edge of the flap and sealed it. "If Brandt's people come to see it ... maybe a knife across your throat."

I looked through the window. The sky was turning gray and leaden, and I felt very tired. A woman with a purple scarf wrapped around her head walked out of a shop.

"All right," I said. "I won't talk to her anymore. Can I go now?"

"Listen," he said, sharply, threatening. "Everything is not so simple. You are interfering with a police matter. And you are endangering your life—I mean it. Where is your passport?"

"In the hotel. In the safe."

"Not anymore." He clicked and unclicked the lock to the door. "Leave Holland in twenty-four hours. The police in the train station are holding your papers. In twenty-four hours. Otherwise we will throw you behind bars for a few weeks before we turn you over to Interpol. Get out."

The dispatcher began squawking over the radio. I pulled the door handle and set a foot on the pavement. The young cop came up to me, grabbed me by the shoulder and hauled me out of the car. He muttered something at me in his dialect, and gave me a shove.

Van Velden rolled down the window halfway, and rested his chin on the edge of the seamed glass.

"Remember, Verlaine. Stay your distance from Jana. This is very serious." He spat and turned away.

The light dome on top of the car began spinning and he engaged the siren. The car pulled sleekly from the curb and sped toward the Museumplein.

In the evening, after dropping off the furs at Frozen Alice, I went to the Leidsestraat and boarded the tram. I punched my farecard and took a seat. Even behind my smoked lenses the bright incandescent lights in the car were unbearable. All the people on board seemed to belong to a dream of another life, sitting quietly with their hands in their laps, neatly and precisely dressed, passing into the future without question.

I made my way to the Rokin and went down a few blocks, my brain racing with sliced-up pictures. Some young soldiers walked by me; they appeared to be NATO troops. They spoke a strange language from the bottom of their throats.

I went into the Great Dane. The air was compressed with hashish and expensive tobacco. I sat at the counter and ordered a black Mexican beer. The bar front gleamed, all chrome and brass, highly polished. The bartender, a haughty young woman, with make-up perfectly applied, took a frosted mug from a small refrigerator and set it down before me.

There was a long mirror behind the bar. It was old with flaws and whorls, and gashes throughout the silvering. The reflection seemed in error, cast in a watery film; the depth of things was heightened, ballooning. I searched its length for a picture of myself. Perhaps it was the angle, a quirk of inattention, the obtusity of its blemishes—but I was nowhere there, and all the rest was configured in a blurring code: a babbling shadow, unrecognizable, unacceptable.

PART II

The train from Dover arrived at Victoria Station late the next evening. I left my suitcase and crate of furs at the luggage check and let myself flow with the crowds streaming down into the Underground.

I rode the train to Leicester Square and walked up into the electric night scene of London. The movie marquees glittered overhead; bouncers in white tuxedos and long sleek overcoats crowded the doorways of the nightclubs. I walked into an arcade lined with eight-foot mirrors. Gangs of Anglo-Saxon youth paraded across the pavement, hairstyle and dress executed precisely to the letter of the code.

I leaned against an iron picket fence. My brain began to reel. There were too many people, there was too much light, all too much. I faded down Coventry Street into Soho, sticking close to the storefronts, glancing quickly into the windows as I flickered by. I saw high-heeled shoes, dinner jackets, and exotic alphabets, and thousand-dollar neon signs that contained but a single word.

I walked on and the rich blood of the terrain began to thin. Shish kebab kiosks began to spring up; there were strange bookshops with blacked-out windows and murky wine bars with garish lights. Three young Egyptians climbed the stairs from a cellar-level cafe. A woman with red lipstick paused beneath a streetlamp to light a cigarette. I followed her into one bar, and then another; dark stout turned to whiskey, the faces changed, floors were tilted; in the streets the headlamps of automobiles shone like nebulae.

I woke up the next morning on a divan in my wife's apartment at Goodge Street. I spent a few minutes studying the arabesques in the tin ceiling before I remembered where I was. I closed my eyes and counted to one hundred in Italian and named as many saints as I could remember.

When I opened my eyes, everything was still there: the walnut bookshelves, the mahogany secretary with panel raised, the portraits of Napoleon and Josephine hanging on the rose-colored walls in swirling rococo frames. I hauled myself up, crossed the Isfahan carpet and peeked into the bedroom.

I barely recognized it. The walls had been repainted in periwinkle. Sunlight crept in around the edges of lace curtains. There was a new bed with four sculpted posts and a strawberry canopy—unslept in.

I went into the kitchen and fried an egg. When I'd finished eating, I washed the dishes and returned to the sitting room. I pulled open the window and looked out over Goodge Street. It was cloudy out, the sky was flannel gray with streaks of black and white: rain threatened.

The air was unseasonably warm and some of the winter birds had come out to sit upon the eaves of the low buildings. A phalanx of people appeared suddenly from around the corner at Charlotte Street. They were armed with umbrellas and briefcases, and several held their overcoats draped over their arms. They threaded their way across the street and towards the Underground, to board the prison trains that carried them to work.

A long navy blue limousine with smoked windows pulled up to the curb opposite. Several odd-shaped aerials—a helix and a trident—jutted up from the boot, and medieval castles were painted in red on the doors.

I remembered a pair of field glasses that hung from a peg in the pantry. I retrieved them, adjusted the diopter and focused in on the vehicle.

The driver's door opened. The chauffeur climbed out and walked around the car. He was attired in a dark green velvet suit, with a black shirt, lizard-skin boots and long white gloves. He was heavily made up, so that he resembled a harlequin.

He jacked open a long door and then another that

swung open in the opposite direction. Inside, two banquettes upholstered in red leather faced each other over a
low onyx table. There was a thick white carpet on the
floor, and two small television screens were bolted to the
roof. Champagne glasses were strewn along the table,
and jade ashtrays were piled high with cigarette butts.

On one of the banquettes, my wife, Claudia Lansdale,
sat next to a man dressed in a leopard-skin suit. He had
long black hair and wore jet-black sunglasses with pink
lenses shaped like hearts. There was no mistaking it was
Trenton Lee, the rock and roll star.

Claudia wore a floor-length ocelot coat with a violet
collar and pearl buttons. A polka-dotted pillbox hat sat
slightly askew atop her pinned-up hair. Because of the
low incline of the banquette, her skirt, short enough as it
was, had pulled up well past her knees. Her long heavenly
legs were veiled in filmy black nylons and Trenton Lee
had a thumb hooked beneath an opalescent garter snap,
his well-manicured, ring-covered fingers splayed across
her inner thigh. The wealthy rocker appeared somewhat
dazed.

Claudia looked back and forth with precision, panning
the imaginary audience that dogged her at every turn.
With a sweeping motion she pushed the hand from her
leg. She daintily extended her arm and allowed the chauffeur to hoist her from the car. With her free hand, she
adjusted the arc of her hat and regally stepped down to
the pavement. She walked across the street, staring this
way and that, minding everything but the traffic, reach-
ing beneath the coat to smooth out the back of her skirt,
stroking it pointedly with the flat of her hand. She was a
heart-stopper, and her price had become too dear for the
likes of me.

I set down the field glasses on a mahogany coffee table,
next to a cigar box painted lime green and decorated with
magical symbols. I sat down in a purple wing-backed
chair. A few minutes later a key turned and Claudia
entered through the door.

She scowled for a second, then wiped her face of all expression. She leaned against a column, stood on one foot and gracefully bent the other back to remove a shoe.

"Hello, Eddie," she said, casually but guardedly. "I wouldn't have thought to find you here."

"You have the key to my flat."

"Oh, that's right—I certainly do." She pushed off the other shoe with her stockinged foot and rested her thumb against her lip. "I think I lent it to Georgie Anne Smith— of the Norwich Smiths—so that she could have an affair in the afternoons with her plumber, or bishop, or voice-coach—I don't remember which."

She unhooked a large kid-leather bag from her shoulder and suspended it from a bronze tree that was screwed to the door. She took off her coat and hung it in a small closet in the anteroom.

"I've just spent the night with Trenton Lee," she said off-handedly. "It was vivid and fabulous... we went to a million parties. There were men with cameras hanging from every chandelier. I've seen more flashbulbs popping of an evening ..."

She turned to me. Absent-mindedly, or so she pretended, she began to unbutton her silk blouse, then stopped midway down. She wore a transparent, pale green camisole underneath, and the sight of her capacious breasts brought to mind the miracles of the Saints.

"And champagne!" she exclaimed. "We drank all that God has created. My goodness."

She placed her hands correctly on her hips and rubbed the bottom of one foot over the top of the other. "But what are you doing here, Eddie? You were meant to be in Amsterdam, laying waste to your mind with black hashish—looking down at Vermeers and Rembrandts, while looking up the skirts of unwitting Dutch women. Were you not?"

I leaned back and drummed my fingers lightly against the sides of the chair. There was no use trying to figure out Claudia, she was so reactive, she rarely understood herself.

"I had to leave a little ... early," I said.

"Are you in straitened circumstances? Have you come to borrow money?" She walked over to the window. Her eyelashes flickered as she regarded all of Goodge Street. "I'm not the local branch of Save the Children, you know ... and why have you left the window open, Eddie? It's absolutely freezing in here. Brr."

She leaned slightly out the window. Her head bobbed about as she studied the motions of the pedestrians. "Why look at that! It's what's his name—that little stink-bomb from the television. Yoo-hoo!" she screamed. "Hey there, hey sucker!"

"Amazing," she said, pulling herself back in and slamming shut the window. "He acted as if he barely knew me, as if I were merely shouting into the wind to exercise my larynx. Maybe he doesn't like girls too much."

"Who could blame him?" I said.

"Naughty, naughty, Eddie." She pulled the pins from her pillbox hat; long brown hair streaked with blonde and gold fell in layers over her shoulders. She stared at me, lowering the lids of her big green eyes until they were just barely slitted open. "But where're your bags?" she said in a flat, slightly taunting voice. "I mean, where are they? Are you playing a trick on me?"

"I left them at Victoria."

She turned and stood stiffly against the edge of the bookcase. Her face was wistful. She drew the corners of her lips down and cocked her head slightly to the side. "You're in trouble aren't you, Eddie?"

"Why do you say that?"

"It's about some furs."

I looked at her sharply. Her face was blank, her eyes looking straight ahead.

"Why do you know about this?"

"A man came by yesterday asking after furs—an awful, awful man." She bit down on her lip. "He said ... he said"—she affected a quaver in her voice—"that you

were meant to sell them at a flystand in the Portobello
Road come Saturday next. He said that you had promised
him a look-see first: 'the right of the first choice' he
called it."

My heart fibrillated. "What was his voice like?"

"It was the voice of evil."

"Come on."

She licked her lips and pressed her hand to her forehead, as if she were searching her memory. "He had a
German accent, perhaps Swiss-German or Black Forest.
His English was precise, but strange, he used several curious turns of phrase, such as I have mentioned. He had an
arresting manner, his eyes were piercing, and I'm sure he
was accustomed to getting his way. A Svengali sort—or
perhaps just a touch mad. But—" She hesitated and
looked at me with a face filled with alarm.

"But what?"

"He was under the curse, Eddie," she said. "I'm not jok-
ing. He didn't care about anything. Not life or death—or
anything in between." She clasped her hands together.
"He frightened me greatly."

"What did you tell him?"

She looked at me indignantly. "Nothing, of course. I
told him that we no longer lived together, and that I
couldn't be expected to have the timetables of every flystand in London. He turned his back and left without saying anything more."

"All right," I said. "Don't worry about it."

Claudia approached me. She had a soft, puzzled look
on her face; I could see that the topic of our conversation
had already dropped from her mind. She knelt down in
front of the chair and rested her cheek on my lap.

"How are the Dutch women in bed, Eddie?" she said in
her most straightforward manner.

"What do you care?"

"Tell Claudia now." She bit down on my leg as hard as
she could. "There's a good little boy." She released her
teeth and climbed up on my lap. She began kissing me on

the neck and toyed at my belt with her fingers. I smelled roses and damp lawns and I let myself sink back, closing my eyes and blackening my brain.

I felt her hand in my pants and she began whispering something in my ear, over and over, like a spell. I began to ascend the ladder, when suddenly she pulled back her head.

"Eddie."

"Yes."

"When we are finished I will draw myself a lovely bath. And you must leave immediately. Your key is in the top drawer of the bureau."

"Okay."

"And don't steal anything."

The key wasn't there, so I lifted fifty quid and went down to the street. I walked north on Tottenham Court Road toward Euston Square. I passed a big bookshop; a poster of the royal family was plastered over and over along the floor of the display window. "Astonishing revelations," said a blurb blown up a hundred power and glued smack over the face of one of the princes. "Gives cause for concern."

I walked down into the Underground at Warren Street. I bought a day ticket and purchased a scandal newspaper. Someone's head had been found inside a refrigerator in East Anglia.

I rode to Earls Court. I threw the paper in the trash can and cleaned my spectacles. I walked up the stairs and found myself in the company of some young lads with Canadian flags sewn into the fabric of their backpacks. They were talking in French, something about cheap hotels.

I followed my shadow down Earls Court Road, past an Indian restaurant and a grocery stall with an orange sign posted out front. The winter sun lit up the frosty breaths of passers-by. Somewhere I'd lost my gloves and I rubbed my hands briskly to keep them warm.

An old dog of mixed parentage nipped at my heels. I touched his shaggy head and he bounded off across the street. I passed a woman wearing a pink turban and blue shoes, and a place called the Hotel Apollo.

At Penywern Road a sign was posted on the brick in florid Arabic. Beneath it said: Gentlemens Clothing. I turned into Earls Court Square. There was Chepstow Hall and the Poetry Society; shipshape rows of trees and empty black benches lined the plaza.

I crossed the square and approached a rust and wine-colored brick building. Bay windows with stained-glass mullions looked out on narrow patios supported by corbels. A walkway sliced through thick cubes of hedge and I ascended three steps inlaid with black and white diamond-shaped stone. I rang the bell at number nine and was let in.

The hallway smelled of cologne. I climbed four flights of stairs. The railing was loose on the third landing, and I took care not to uproot the balusters. At the top of the staircase I turned right and stopped at the second apartment. A vivid color cartoon of Daisy Duck performing an unspeakable act on a sepia-toned Joseph Stalin was painted on the door. The apartment was unlocked and I walked in.

Inside was a vast room painted top to bottom in blinding white. The joists of the ceiling were exposed and the floorboards were rough-hewn and coarsely sanded, so that it seemed to be the bow of a freshly painted ancient ship. The room was empty of furnishing, save for a few overstuffed ottomans, and a small cot. An inverted Union Jack hung from the sill beneath the shutters of the bay.

In the middle of the room a man stood in front of an easel staring at an empty canvas. He wore a white T-shirt, white wool pants and high-topped sneakers without insignia. His head was shaven bald, and he had a Fu Manchu mustache that had been bleached white, and rose eerily from his black face, like a crescent of the moon. He wore no socks, but had tattooed or painted white bracelets around his ankles.

"What are you doing, Parker?"

"I'm studying the canvas," he replied without looking at me. "It's unusually silent for a miserable piece of cloth."

"You don't know what you're going to paint?"

"Of course I know what I'm going to paint," he said impatiently. He picked a piece of lint off the muslin and flicked it over his shoulder. "I've prepared several, precise exploratory sketches. It will be called 'St. Mark Preaching to the Masses at Times Square.' But I can't get started, you know, until I've located the genius, or the genie, if you will, of the canvas itself. Everything in the universe, be it animate or inanimate, or otherwise, has an epicenter, a source of energy. And only a pisshead deals with anything until it is located."

I went up and looked over his shoulder. He wore studded earrings shaped like crucifixes and his neck smelled of sandalwood soap.

"What's with all the white?"

"The white—the fabulous, evil white? You want to know about it?" He turned and looked at me. He opened his eyes wide, and they seemed ready to pop from his head. "It's a statement. It's the word."

"Which is?"

He shrugged and turned his palms up. They were bright pink and inscribed in ball point pen with algebraic formulae. He swept his eyes back and forth, as if he were watching something racing along the wainscoting. "I don't know, I'm not quite sure. I need a little more time to give it proper shrift. It has something to do with the white season of Christmas—the x, the cross, the daughter of the ankh of ancient Egypt. It has to do with Dali's visions of Vermeer, the search for the materials, unknown to us, that produced the startling whites of the pallets at Delft ... It has to do with white shit, white vomit, the leukocytes, the harbingers of death of the blood ..."

"All that?"

"All that—to the final power. Of course, I could be

wrong." He picked up a small tin of varnish, dipped a brush into it and began lacquering the canvas. "And that," he continued, "would be only slightly better than being right. Do you have any money?"

"Forty-nine quid," I said, turning my head: the smell of the varnish was overpowering.

"No thanks, then. I need some real money."

"What for?"

He screwed the lid back on the varnish and set it on the floor. He cupped his hand around his ear and held it an inch from the canvas. "Do you hear it?" he asked. "It's the unmistakable call of the epicenter. The bottomless whirl-wind ... it's like the singing of the sirens."

He pulled a grease pencil from his pocket and began frantically lining something into the muslin. "Why do I need money, Edward? I need it for drugs and women and alcohol. Nothing else of any import is very expensive, is it?" He looked at me with disbelief. He waved the grease pen in zigzags, looked at some point on his fingernail and shook his head.

"I may be forced to sell a painting. Some asshole in Brussels has offered me thirty-five thousand pounds for *St. Sebastian on the Floor of the Chicago Grain Exchange.*"

"That will buy something."

"Thirty-five is a bad number. I only deal in multiples of threes. The troika, the Trinity." He smiled, showing two rows of teeth too white to be real. A ruby, inset in the lower left bicuspid, caught a ray of light and gleamed at me. "The three prongs of Neptune's fork, the third son, Seth: life at the end of death, do you hear me. The bastard should have stopped at thirty-three ... He's a chandler of weapons and armaments, cleaned up on the Falklands thing ... his death-dollars are bad enough luck as it is..."

I followed him through an archway into the kitchen. Everything was dazzling white: the breakfast counter and the cane chairs beneath it, the handles of the drawers, the plates and saucers stacked in the breakfront.

Parker opened the refrigerator. All the cans and cartons inside were painted white. He produced two white bottles of beer, kicked shut the door and removed the bottle-caps with his teeth.

"Where've you been keeping yourself, Eddie?"

"I've been in Holland."

He took a long slug of beer and looked at the ceiling. "Of that I know," he said. "I had a run-in with your old wife one evening about Sloane Square. And strikingly laid-out she was, with a little green skirt that showed the hems of her knickers. She informed me of your travels... She's been whoring off with some rock stars, you know?"

"Yeah."

Parker rested a hand on my shoulder and looked me square in the eyes. "A fine lad you are, Eddie, and an outstanding way you have with the skirts—but you're not much likely to further advance the career of a young actress hungry for fame."

"I guess not."

"There's really no guesswork involved." He removed the grease pencil from his pocket and began scribbling over the notes inked on his palm. His lips moved soundlessly and he shook his head, negating something. "I was in Amsterdam two years ago last Guy Fawkes Day. The women are a bit on the plain side, but smashingly dressed to compensate, aren't they? And outside of Hamburg, one of the most spectacular breed of prostitutes in the Western world." He smiled, took in a deep breath and triumphantly exhaled. "The chemicals are as pure as mother's milk, and you can stand tall and smoke cannabis in the bars like a man, not a cowering animal. Is that not so?"

I nodded my head. I noted that my temples were aching. It was from the glare.

"There's too much white, Parker," I said.

"Oh no, sir," he remonstrated. He pushed his hands against an imaginary wall. "You're dead wrong. It's only the very beginning of white."

"What do you mean?"

"I mean"— he raised his hands slowly in the air—"that white never ends. It travels along the surface of an expanding sphere. The day of white, the season of white, the apocalyptic serpentine progression of fucking bleeding white. White never ends—I swear it."

We stood there drinking for a few minutes without speaking. My heart was beating irregularly, a film of sweat rolled over my forehead. Parker was deep in thought, his eyes closed, his fingers locked and pressed lightly against his belly.

"So what is it then, Eddie?" he said presently, opening his eyes.

"I need you to come along with me to Victoria to pick up a bag."

"I see." He pressed a fingertip to the cleft of his chin. "Some trouble?"

"I don't know."

Parker walked over to the counter and looked carefully at a large piece of ivory that was fastened to the wall. He felt it with his hand as if he were taking its temperature. "Well, shall we go then?"

"Yes."

"Shall I bring my cane?"

"The Malaysian?"

"The very one."

"Bring it."

We walked down Earls Court Road and turned right onto Old Brompton. We passed a coffee house—men in black leather jackets were smoking cigarettes and chalking billiard-cues. We went past a vegetable store, an Asian travel bureau and a shop without a sign where a man was rubbing black paint on a picture frame.

We came to the entrance of the Brompton Cemetery. We passed through a black metal gate beneath a stone archway and past two cupids holding bows. It had begun to snow, and a light dust sprinkled the grounds. There was still a haze of sun behind the clouds, putting everything in a bright gray light.

Parker carried the cane wedged beneath his left armpit, leaving him to gesture with his right hand only. He pointed a finger at a crypt adorned with Coptic crosses.

"What must it be like, Eddie, to be kept underground among the glowworms and the loam—without friend or foe?" he asked. He took a deep breath and blew it out, creating a great cloud of vapor.

"I can't imagine it," I said.

"Burial?"

"No. Death."

We walked up the stairs of a mausoleum and stopped before a rusted green gate. Inside we saw a cross attached to wheels and a stone angel kneeling before a tomb. An inscription next to the gate read: He only sleepeth.

Parker put down his cane and grabbed onto the iron pickets. "We can rage against it," he said in a loud voice, shaking the gate. "We can voice all manner of protest and disbelief ... But to what end? It visits us each and all as surely as the moon wanes and waxes."

We walked down the steps and continued on the path. In the distance a church rose from behind a forest; it was decked with fortifications, like a castle of the Middle Ages. We came to another massive crypt. We descended to a vestibule and stopped before two high metal doors that were chained together and padlocked. The iron was embossed with a pair of snakes wrapped around a pole. Beneath them a third snake circumscribed a winged hourglass and was devouring its own tail.

The top halves of the doors were jalousied; we squinted and looked through the slats. As our eyes adjusted to the dark, we made out a deep dank room piled with rotting leaves. To either side there were rows of shelves embedded in the walls, housing rusted caskets. In the center of the room there was a sea-green iron bell with an eagle perched atop it, a group of angels, and many strange-shaped crosses.

"This is it, old man," said Parker. He tapped at the ground with his cane. "This is the end of the line ... Funny, what?" He turned and looked at me, his eyes bulging. "Yes, it's a funny thing," he repeated. "Our minds can comprehend the workings of subatomic particles, we have observed the moons of Saturn with our rockets, we can cure syphilis and smallpox with ease. But after five million years our comprehension of death is unchanged one iota. We have the syrupy fairy tales of the church, and the dismal blackness of the unbeliever to choose from, and no one ever returns to enlighten us any further."

We turned from the chambers and walked on among the stones and graves. Parker produced an alabaster cigarette case from inside his coat; he flicked a catch with his thumb and the top sprung open. He proffered the box; I extracted a portly hand-rolled cigarette and stuck it between my lips.

He shrouded a lighter with his hand to shield it from the blowing snow. We passed a black headstone engraved with Masonic symbols. The snow became heavier and the glaze of the sun disappeared. I inhaled deeply on the cigarette to take the fire; it tasted slightly bitter, of opium and, more sweetly, of hashish. I watched the changes in the color gradation of the scenery as the smoke passed through my alveoli and into my bloodstream.

"Life is a miracle," I said.

"Yes," said Parker, taking the cigarette from me and staring at its dull ember. "It redeems itself, doesn't it? The gift of thought is better than life everlasting. It's as far as I can get."

We walked to the end of the path. The sun edged out again momentarily. We took a last look back; the floor of the cemetery was white and crystalline. We turned and walked through an archway. We passed a red telephone booth and were at the corner of Fulham Road and Gunter Grove.

At Victoria we pushed through the mobs and stood in the

queue at the luggage check. There were about thirty people in front of us, and only one clerk on duty, an old doddering man.

"He appears to be either deaf or blind," said Parker.

We moved along at a snail's pace. I glanced around nervously, feeling claustrophobic—and a nearly total loss of perspective. In front of us, two teen-aged girls in floridly embroidered jeans discussed something in animated Spanish.

"*Es de putamadre, tía. Maravillosa.*"

"*Qué rollo.*"

I looked at Parker. He was serene, the creases in his face dissolved, his eyes clear and focused straight ahead. "I have to get some air," I told him.

"All right. Give me the claim check."

I went back out the front entrance, and walked around the corner to Buckingham Palace Road. A bum grabbed an abandoned baggage cart and tried to pose as a porter before some suitcase-laden tourists struggling towards Eccleston Bridge. I bought some strawberries at a fruit stand set up along the wall and slowly ate them, leaning against the embankment over the train yard, watching the sons of man streaming up and down the road.

I felt apprehensive about everything. I heard people arguing but I didn't look up at them, or move close enough to get the details. I re-entered the station through a dim, seldom used entrance. I walked along a green corridor lit with fluorescent bulbs and papered with old advertisements.

I went back out into the body of the station, caught up again in the great hubbub. I approached the baggage claim, looking at the awning of Boots Dispensing Chemists. Two adults and three children carrying suitcases ran past me at full speed.

I gazed up at the middle of the queue but I could not see Parker. I looked to the front. A sign said 'Left Luggage, Items £1.50. Walking (or shooting) Stick, Bobsleigh, Oars (per pair), Holdall, Hockey Stick.' I realized that they had changed attendants. I kept looking for Parker, my heart pounding, and then I saw that he was first in line and that the new clerk, a young efficient-looking man, was returning to the scratched-up wood counter, holding the box of furs in his hands, my suitcase already resting at Parker's side.

I caught something happening out of the corner of my eye, and I turned to look to my left. From behind the white hexagonal cubicle where they give out information came Ralph from the flea market. He was cleanly shaved, hair cut short and neatly parted. He was wearing a cheap blue suit, with shirt and tie and polished shoes.

As Parker pulled the box from the cylinders on the counter, Ralph picked up his pace and began striding towards him. He had one hand stuck inside his jacket, as if he were holding something. Then he moved faster yet, ready to break into a sprint.

He didn't see me running towards him until the last moment. His face registered astonishment as I raised my hands and shoved him as hard as I could into the pedestal of a blue and yellow column.

He bounced off it and rolled to the ground. I grabbed the lapel of his jacket, pulled it back and kicked him in the head. He was holding a Walther automatic in his hand.

"Help! Police!" I yelled. "Someone with a gun here! Help!"

The crowd assisted me; people began screaming and diving for the floor. Ralph, dazed and bleeding from the ear, kept the gun hugged to his chest. His eyeballs rolled faintly behind slitted lids. His diaphragm swelled and he shuddered, his lungs struggling to purchase some air. I walked away as a herd of policemen came running towards the scene.

In the confusion, Parker had managed to nab someone's baggage cart; I spotted him wheeling my luggage at moderate speed towards the Victoria Street passageway. I caught up and followed behind him at fifteen yards. No sooner had he gone through the door when more police moved in and sealed off the entrance.

Immediately a nervous crowd began to aggregate in front of the police line. More shouting came from the direction where Ralph had fallen, everything seemed out of focus, everyone's face stiffened with panic. A stout, bespectacled old woman, her chin and hands sprouting hair and covered with warts began shrieking at one of the policemen, demanding to be let out of the station.

"The gun!" I said.

All hell broke loose; the crowd began to riot. It was only passingly difficult to slip around the cop at the edge of the line as he struggled to maintain order with the end of his truncheon.

I shoved through the next wave of people angrily trying to push their way into the station. I made it to daylight.

I walked past the crowds and stood on the curb. Parker was standing across the way in one of the bus queues. He looked calm and unapprehensive, standing tall and smoking a cigarette, his cane rested against the baggage cart, his black shaven head rising spectrally from the white fox collar of his coat. We caught each other's eyes but made no gestures of recognition.

It was at that moment that I felt as if my nose was filling with blood, and it seemed certain that I was the center of the universe, like the earth before Copernicus, and that all that I saw — the huge red buses, the gabled theatre, the hordes of mankind, the trash cans and telephone booths — one and all were revolving about me like asteroids and planets, caught in the locus of my gravity, following my path across time.

I remembered all my dreams: sitting in the utmost rows of stadiums watching the distant performances: trying desperately to flee while my feet became bogged down in an unaccountable mire, my legs leaden; looking at my watch and realizing that I had missed the same appointment over and over; my mother screaming at me that the school bus was waiting at the corner.

I felt something in my back, dug in painfully beneath

the fifth vertebrae. Someone whispered in my ear. "Don't move now, Eddie—now is not the time. Do as I say or I will blow your kidneys to Piccadilly Circus ... Cross the street with me—you see that green Mercedes waiting at the curb—"

We walked in tandem off the sidewalk and across the pavement. I watched Parker; he was not looking in my direction, nor did he seem concerned about me. He was staring down at his shoes, and resting one hand atop the box of furs. I lost sight of him as we walked around the back of a bus.

There was a long queue waiting to board; we had to push our way through. It opened quickly to let us pass then snapped shut again like a man-eating plant. A large fellow with a goatee and horn-rimmed spectacles climbed out of the Mercedes. A plaid overcoat was buttoned tightly at his neck; he wore shiny gray boots and kid gloves. He held open the back door as I spotted Parker again.

"Don't break, now," said the voice in my ear. "You must signal to your friend, then climb into the car. Do not portray your true feelings on your face, or I will kill you in a second." I felt the sharp prodding at my spine.

I waved at Parker, finally catching his eye. He began wheeling the cart towards us. I got into the car—the motor was running, and the smell of cigar smoke was mixed with the fumes of the exhaust. Werner followed me in.

"God help you if you turn your head," he muttered, "and pray to his son, Jesus, that there are no fuck-ups."

The large man slammed shut the door and ran across the bus lanes toward Parker, the tails of his plaid coat ruffling in the air. Parker looked up nonchalantly, then began pushing the cart full speed right at him. The man opened his hands, trying to break his stride. Parker clipped him in the knees. The cart flipped over, the box spilled out; the man stumbled, but held his balance.

Parker gripped his cane and released the bayonet at the

tip. He began slashing at the man, cutting ribbons in the sleeves of his coat; a red stain appeared at the shoulder.

I clenched my jaw and started to turn my body. "Hold still," said Werner. The sharp thing was in my rib cage now. I looked down and saw a small-caliber revolver with a blued handle. The people in the queues began running across Victoria Street; the bus doors slammed shut. With three successive motions of his hands, quick enough to catch flies midair, the goateed man grabbed at Parker's stick and wrested it away. He raised his leg and snapped the cane in two over his knee. He dropped the pieces to the ground and picked up the box from the sidewalk.

Parker lunged at him, grabbing for the throat, but quick as a weasel, the man turned at the last second and knocked Parker across the chest with the box, sending him hurtling to the ground. The man raised the box over his head and sprinted back to the car.

Werner climbed over the seat, keeping the gun pointed at my face. He pushed a button on the dash and the trunk sprang open. His crony threw in the box and slammed shut the trap. His arms were covered in blood but he didn't seem to notice.

He pulled open the door and climbed in next to me. Werner tossed him the gun, threw the Mercedes in gear and went careening over the curb and down the sidewalk. He shot out past a horrified taxi driver and went back down over the curb onto Wilton Road. He pounded on the horn and sent thirty people racing for higher ground.

I looked behind and saw Parker running after us, his face still enigmatic and unreflecting. His great white coat came unbuttoned and flared open in the wind, and he looked like a huge heron sailing across the sidewalk.

Werner steered the car around a fishmonger's truck and turned onto Gillingham Street. He slowed down somewhat and began speaking in a soft German dialect. The big man nodded and removed his jacket, one side at a time, keeping the gun trained on me. He balled the jacket up and pushed it against the wound on his left shoulder.

He smiled. The thickness of the glass in his spectacles was nearly half an inch.

We passed a bus garage and the Eccleston Hotel. It was covered with big red canopies and ornamented with bushes and an iron gate.

"What language is that?"

I watched Werner's reflection in the rear view mirror, and he looked there for me. His gaunt face was shaven clean as polished stone; his eyes were deadly-green with pupils small as pin-pricks. He wore a pale gray necktie over a stiffly-starched white shirt; even the points of his collar were ironed sharp as metal.

"Our language? It's Swiss-German," he said, looking away from the mirror. A bellman stepped out onto the pavilion of the hotel and lit a cigarette.

"Why do you pretend to be German if you are Swiss?'

Werner took a silk handkerchief from his breast pocket and dabbed at his lips. He accelerated the car as we passed into Belgravia.

"Easy to blame those Germans," he said. "No one expects the bastards to be up to much good, do they? Let them make the wars, while we make the money..."

"The war was a long time ago," I said.

"Forty years is not long—it is a second. The bell-tower in the center of Bern, our capital, is eleven hundred years old. The clock on it still works ..."

We turned right, into a quiet street and then right again through a stone archway into a mews. There was a row of small quaint houses, all of different colors, light pink, ivory, plum and buff. Werner picked up a remote control panel from the seat and pressed his thumb on a diamond-shaped black button. He pulled sharply into a narrow drive and went beneath the lip of a garage door that was rolling back electronically, and down a sharp incline.

We drove into a vast underground lot, dimly lit from above with fluorescent tubes. There were several cars parked there, spaced apart at wide and irregular distances, like pieces left on the board at the end of a chess game.

We pulled up parallel to an old green Bentley. Werner turned off the ignition and pushed a switch to let down the windows. There was an intense quiet and the light in the lot was of a greenish hue, so that it seemed that we were on a surface as distant and strange as the moon. Werner turned around and looked at us. He smiled with closed lips, first at me, then at his accomplice. "Well— here we are."

The man with the goatee cleared his throat. "What shall we do now?" he said in lucid English.

Werner shrugged his shoulders. "We must destroy the world."

"It is already destroyed," said the other man.

"Yes, you are right, Klaus." He scratched his head. "Then perhaps we must glue back together a few of the pieces ..."

"So we can destroy it again ..."

They both began laughing maniacally. "Yes," said Werner, wiping a tear from his eye, "so we can destroy it once again."

The laughter stopped and the quiet returned. I stared out the window. The green of the light grew sharper, the air was dank and I could smell the moist blood. I looked at Werner's cutting features, his face tinted by the lamps, and I felt as if I were inside a reptile house, waiting for something to happen that I could not imagine.

The man removed his shirt. There was a huge laceration on the left shoulder, but the blood had clotted fairly well around it. Werner opened the glove compartment and removed a half liter of blended Scotch. He poured some on the henchman's wound. He returned the bottle, took the bloodied shirt and ripped it into strips, and wrapped the shoulder with it.

Werner took the gun and put it in his pocket. He pushed the button on the dash and the trunk sprang open, startling me. "You must take care of the car, Klaus. And of yourself."

He opened the door. "Come with me, Eddie. I do not
know what to do with you now. You are fortunate, for I
know you have no code of honor, even less than myself.
That may save you yet. Meanwhile you can carry the box
for me."

"All right." I got out of the car.

We walked across the lot, and came to a steel wall.
Werner depressed a glowing red lozenge and the doors of
an elevator pulled open. We stepped onto a green carpet
and the doors clapped shut. Two of the interior panels
were mirrored, the other two were made of chrome. They
were joined at irregular angles, so that the mirrors
reflected over and over, the last discernible image shrink-
ing us to the size of postage stamps. The light overhead
was bright and relentless, and as we shot upwards it
seemed like we were traveling into the distant future.

The elevator doors opened and we entered a hallway.
The walls were papered with fox-hunting scenes, pieces
of dark Victorian furniture were set up along the wall.
We walked to the left, passing doors marked with brass
numerals. Our footsteps were soundless on the thick
carpet.

Werner stopped before number thirty-nine. "Open the
door."

I let go of the box and tried the knob. Werner elbowed
me aside and pushed the door open with his foot. In the
middle of the room there was a round bed. It was spread
with a pink and blue coverlet, with tassels hanging along
the purl. There were two windows on the far wall, the curtains drawn closed. The room was lit with two brass
lamps that stood at either side of the bed.

To the right, pushed against the wall, stood an old
mahogany dressing table. An oval mirror, the silvering
spotted, was suspended above it in a spindled bracket. In
front of it, set at an angle, there was a matching bench,
and upon it sat Jana. She was smoking a cigarette and had
one leg crossed over the other.

She considered us coolly. She held the filter of the cigarette affectedly between her thumb and index finger, as if she were demonstrating a jewel. She was different: her hair was dyed pinkish-blonde, braided in the manner of the Rastafarians, and she wore round sunglasses with red lenses. She had on a midnight blue kid-leather jerkin that laced up the front, revealing the orbs of her breasts; a short velvet skirt; opaque stockings trimmed with sequins; and scarlet shoes with silver buckles, yellow bows and sharp heels wrapped with tin foil.

"Hello, Eddie," she said. She smiled curtly, bemused. "How are you doing this day?"

"Okay. Yourself?"

Jana rested the cigarette on a rose-tinted ashtray on the vanity. She turned on a pinup lamp and studied the tiny flowers painted on her nails.

"I saw a picture of your wife in a magazine," she said. "She's very pretty."

With a small penknife, Werner began unscrewing the planking that enclosed the box. He worked slowly, methodically, placing the screws in a neat pile, stacking the slats one atop the other on the carpet. He cut open the tape on top that fused the flaps, and bent back the cardboard. One at a time, he pulled out the furs, counting the buttons—one, two, three, four, five—then laid them on the floor.

The sixth coat had only four buttons.

He took the pelt and spread it out over the coverlet. He smoothed the arms and meticulously adjusted the collar, then fluffed out the pelt with his fingertips.

"Fit for a king, wouldn't you say," remarked Werner, reverentially, his eyes appearing to glisten. "Yes ... Jackpot."

With a long smooth stroke he slit the bottom of the coat beneath the hem. He grabbed at a string and pulled out a long intestine-shaped plastic bag.

"Hello, gorgeous," he said to the bag, running his hand along it. "Yes—this is very beautiful. You have serviced us nicely, Eddie. You are a fine donkey."

Jana's eyebrows hopped up and down beneath the red lenses. She looked from the bed to the floor and back again. She uncrossed her legs and locked her hands between her knees.

"Please, Eddie," she said, "you must leave the room ... You may sit in the hallway for a few minutes. Werner?"

He barely paid attention. "Yes ... of course." He deliberated over the words. He coiled the bag like a long white sausage. "But don't try to go anywhere. All the roads lead to hell... We don't like runaways."

I went into the corridor. Behind me, the door slammed shut, a key turned and a bolt snapped. I walked down the passageway until I reached a casement window. I tried to pull it up, but it was nailed shut.

I stood there for several minutes watching it grow dark through the glass. The street lights went on, and a soft yellow corona enveloped the sash of the window. I went back to number thirty-nine and knocked. I received no reply. The door came open.

Jana was sitting at the edge of the bed, hands folded, head slightly bowed. The skin of her face was flushed and her make-up was smutted at the corners of her eyes. There was no trace of Werner, or the furs, or the long plastic tubing.

"Come sit down next to me, Eddie," she said in a distant voice. "You can tell me a story from the sea, or a memory of some ghosts." Slowly she raised her head. Her lips were slanted down, and her eyes looked sharply to the left. "Tell me, do you understand what is happening around us?"

I took a place beside her on the rounded quilt. I filled with anger, I wanted to grab her by the hair and pull her head back. "Yes, I understand," I said. "You've had me smuggle a pound of heroin into England."

Jana thought for a moment. She opened her eyes; the pupils looked swollen. She put a finger to her lips and pushed out the tip of her tongue. "Oh, no. Who cares about that? That's all about Werner, the game he plays—

with you, with me, with everyone. Anyway, it's no more, it's done, it's dust on the floor ... we must sweep it under the carpets."

"Why are you here then?"

"That's what I'm asking you, Eddie." She grabbed my hand. Her palm was cold and soft, very dry. She dug her nails between my knuckles. "Why am I here, Eddie. I am not tired enough of it yet? Why aren't we dreaming instead? Why aren't we dead? Why me, why me ... what's wrong, what is wrong ... why am I caught in my body like a rat in the iron cage?" Her nails pulled at my skin like a claw. "Help me someone."

All the lights in the room were on; the two lamps flanking the bed, the overhead bulbs, two sconces glowing above the dressing table. But the room seemed dark like an alley—everything cast in shadows—Jana's sadness painted the walls and ceiling, until I felt myself changing color as well, a gray mist creeping over me.

"Where's Werner?"

"He's gone. He has a problem."

"What's that?"

"You must ask him, not me. I tell you, this is not my game." She let go of my hand and peered at the curtained window across the room. "You do not like the heroin, do you, Eddie?"

"No," I said hoarsely, "I don't. It brings bad luck, and worse than that, bad company."

"But it kills the pain."

"No, that's not true," I said. "It only kills the time of the pain."

She looked at me then, with a look of surprise, as if she'd never seen me before. She shook her head: her earrings, long cobalt triangles, three to a lobe, rattled against one another like tinny dice spitting from the cup.

"That is very smart to say, Eddie. That is very smart. Finally you show me something ..." Jana shut her eyes tightly, and locked her fingers against her temples. "The time of the pain passes, not noticed, but the pain has been there all the same"—she spoke slowly, hypnotically—"making its record in your brain. It can never be erased...only delayed a minute ... an hour ... a year ... before it comes back again to bite." She opened her eyes.

She put her arms around my neck, and placed her cheek on my shoulder. I smelled her perfume and something burning, an aroma from her treated hair. "Don't leave me, Eddie," she said softly. She pulled me tighter and everything was covered in a glowing fog.

I raised my hands and touched her shoulders. I tried to push her back against the bed. She resisted me, clutching me around the neck, and pushing her nose into my cheek. "No, Eddie," she said. "I don't know what to do."

She curled her head, undulating like a cat. Her throat was cold, her ears hot.

"What's wrong?"

"What I want," she whispered thickly, "it's too far inside of me to come out. It makes a chain around me. Do you understand?" She pressed her lips to my collar. I felt her breath against my larynx.

"I think so."

"Jana is goddess of the light and dark," she said dryly, "but also of the gates and the doors. In the winter I am January—can you look inside me and see the lights hiding, Eddie?"

"I'm trying."

She loosed her grip, then pulled at me, guiding me down in a slow wobbling arc until we lay on our sides on the bedspread, our feet still on the ground. I pressed my mouth to the edge of her lips; the gloss upon them tasted of wax and apricots. She did not pull away.

"Eddie, no," she murmured. "I'm lost ... I don't know what. It's dark, it's dark. My gate is shutting on the black fire."

"It doesn't matter," I said. I let my fingers feather along her waist. "The sun will come again tomorrow. It always does."

"No," she said, grievingly. "Tomorrow is always night."

We were soundless. She pushed herself closer, shivering. She rolled on top, digging her knees against me. She edged her fingers between my legs, and began biting on my neck. I undid the lacing on her jerkin and my tongue glissaded around her aureoles; she had my johnson in her hand—she made it feel like the staff of Zeus. She raised her skirt, and probed with me, finally plunging it in as if she were spearing a fish. She began fighting with me, pounding at me with her fists, and I had to pin her wrists to continue.

"No, no, no! Eddie. It must not happen! The ocean is too black, I can't breathe, I'm drowning... I'm drowning."

I was in the changing angle; I closed my eyes and saw the edges shifting, hard to soft. Jana convulsed with her legs as I hit the crescendo and it was clear and almost painful and all the surfaces returned, and I was imprisoned in her night.

I went into the bathroom and turned on the light. The walls were tiled in pale green marble, the floor in white diamonds. A blue silk curtain was pulled across the tub, a black bathmat lay in front of it. An oval mirror with a water-gilded frame was bolted in above a small porcelain sink with glittering faucets of brass.

There was a faint smell of cigarette smoke and butane. I glanced at myself in the looking glass, my skin was blurred and underexposed. The darkened lenses caused me to appear like a masked highwayman, and then a raccoon, and my long hair was that of a woman. I ran water from the bidet and splashed myself with it. I dried with a purple towel and hitched up my trousers.

I stepped on the black mat and pulled back the curtain over the tub. The bath was drawn and Margo was lying in the water, her chin and nose barely above the surface. She had no clothes on, and was lovely to look at; her face serene as the gates of heaven, her breasts swollen and vivid. She wore a strand of pearls around her neck, and her hair was fixed up on top with silver barrettes. Her eyes were just barely closed; I couldn't tell if she was dead.

I leaned over and touched her neck. It was cool and I felt for the artery. Suddenly the door swung open. I turned my head and saw Werner's face in the mirror. He was wearing a gray Stetson cowboy hat, a string tie was fastened at his neck with a turquoise stay.

"Hey, come!" He took me brusquely by the shoulder and spun me around. "You must get out of here now." He grabbed my collar and pushed me out the door, slamming it shut. I waved my right hand in his face, and slammed my left fist into his stomach. He looked surprised for a moment. He sent his knee into my groin, laced his hands together, pulled them back over his shoulder and slammed them across the side of my jaw. I went flying against the wall.

I sat there shaking my head, trying to chase out the ringing bells. Werner looked at me and started laughing. "You are some dumb fuck, Eddie," he said. "Do you think I'm going to fight fair?" He grabbed me by the lapels of my shirt and raised me to my feet. Everything had red spots printed across it. I looked at the bed; Jana was gone.

Werner pushed his face within an inch of my own. I stared back at him. His eyes were lucid as glass, the green irises shimmering, ready to float off the white sockets. Smelling of garlic and fragrant tobacco, he smiled; the diamond in his tooth glittered.

"Eddie, my friend. We're in, maybe, a little too deep? Yes ...?" He stepped down on my foot, clamping my boot to the rug. I looked past his shoulder, at the wall. The red spots expanded and began to move about like amoebas.

"What do you say, friend?" He let go of my shirt and slapped me across the mouth with the back of his hand. "Do you want to say some prayers?"

He slapped me again and pushed me against the wall. "Come on, sucker! Tell me fast! What do you believe? Who is your God? Tell me."

I didn't understand what to say. I closed my eyes and saw a grid of electric lines, a pattern graven into the brain, violet and yellow neon lines, a map of something pointing to the end of days, what else could we be following.

"Tell me, tell me, tell me you asshole—who is God? Tell me or you are dead meat!"

I opened my eyes. Over his shoulder there was a copy of a painting hung on the wall: Ophelia's head bobbing on top of a river.

"Who is it!" he screamed. Everything was shifting, sand in the desert, the amoebas splitting and merging, swallowed by the paramecium, our foreheads dissolving.

"My God is dead," I said. "What do you care?"

There was a twitch in his face; his nose flared and the cilia at the rims of the nostrils appeared to stiffen. He let go of me and stared at the backs of his hands as he lowered them to his sides.

"My God is alive," he said quietly. "But He is not good— He is mostly bad. He does not love but He is loved. He is not invisible—no. He is green ... He is not dead, He is alive. He lives in the wallet, He lives in the bank. He brings a slow painful death to those who do not have Him."

He removed a patterned billfold from a vest pocket and pulled out a sheaf of hundred-dollar bills. He pushed them against his mouth and began kissing them as if they were the hands of every beautiful woman who had ever lived. Hesitatingly, with a reluctant rueful look, he returned the bills to their pouch.

"So much for the theology, Eddie. My grandfather was a priest of Luther in the canton of Lucerne ... He committed suicide in the week that the Nazis crossed into Norway. He said that God had betrayed him ..."

He turned from me and began to pace the floor while he ground his palms together. "We have some problems here, Eddie," he said, in a familiar tone. "Perhaps you have some suggestion." He stopped suddenly and stared at a spot in a far imaginary distance. "Are you wondering why I am unloading this weight in England, and not Holland?"

"Yes."

"I will tell you," he said with force. "I do not like to shit in my own bed, do you understand? I am too well known in Amsterdam. The police are following with too much interest everything I do. When I wake up in the morning, I find them sleeping next to me. It would be a long life behind the iron bars if they caught me dealing in white Burmese ... But in England, I am not so famous, and besides the market here is inflated—I can knock down, maybe double, maybe triple the price. When we heard you were coming we could not resist ..."

He took the Stetson off his head and smoothed down the networks of the feather in the brim. His eyes started blinking rapidly, as if a message was being telegraphed from his unconscious.

He spoke in a low voice: "I had the deal set up ... Shit— it was very good, so excellent. Klaus was to deliver the entire weight—lock, stock and barrel—yes ... to one man in St. John's Wood. Beautiful, a single shot, weigh and pay and bang we're gone."

He turned towards me and positioned the hat on his head. "Last night, while I was sleeping on the train coming down from Glasgow, this man ... the one-trick fence ... is going from the eighth floor window of his hotel down to the sidewalk. You see, not using the stairs, or the elevator. Very strange. Very dead."

"Fell or jumped?"

"Or was pushed."

"Are you involved?"

"No!" he exploded. "Absolutely not." His face reddened, his features distorted, he blew a jet of air disgustedly from his lips. "We don't know why it happened, nor do we want to. Only the philosophers and the women must understand everything ... It's a dangerous business—that's why it pays so much. The little fish, if they're brave, can swim with the big."

He looked at me with a half-amused smile. There was a momentary lapse in the electricity, all the lamps blinked off and on. "This weight is worth a fortune. It is pure, very pure—sixty percent. We could step on it six times and still kill half the junkies in London. Right now, wholesale, without touching it, half a million dollars. Not much to the Rockefellers, but to fellows like you and I, Eddie ... eh?"

Before I had a chance to respond there came a staccato rapping on the door. Werner froze, and put a finger to his lips. He drew the revolver from his coat and trained it at the source of the sound. The rapping came again, louder, more frenetic. In the hall someone was yelling in an unintelligible language.

Werner hastened to the door. He pulled back the lock with his free hand. The door flew open and Klaus was there holding a semi-automatic pistol, waving it madly with his hands, cursing and imploring.

Werner made a quick reply. I understood that Klaus was to go prepare the car. He turned and I heard him running down the hallway, and the sound of a heavy door opening and footsteps racing down a stairway. Werner dropped to the floor and went fishing beneath the bed. He fastened onto something and came to his knees pulling out an alligator-hide attaché case, with brass latches and a black lacquered handle.

The gun-hand was braced against the floor. I stomped on his fingers, he yelped and released the weapon. He was slightly off-balance; I shoved him over and picked up the gun. I stepped back two spaces and pointed it at him.

"I'll kill you, you bastard!" he screamed.

"No, you won't."

"You'll have to shoot me through the forehead to get this."

"I don't want it," I said. "It's bad luck. Hurry up and go."

Werner got to his feet. He held the attaché case so tightly that his knuckles whitened, but otherwise he was all composed again. He ran his fingers deftly across his forehead, and adjusted the stay of his string tie. "Give me back my gun," he said, looking me squarely in the eyes.

"No."

"Then what do I owe you?"

"I owe you nothing," I said. "You owe me nothing. Where's Jana?"

He shrugged his shoulders. "Let go of it, man. It's not in the cards for you anymore. She's a witch, and her magic is too strong. Don't you see? She has the sign between her eyes. Now give me my gun."

I extended my arm and pulled the trigger. There was a deafening roar; the mirror above the dressing table exploded in a hundred thousand shards of twinkling glass. Werner looked at me as if he'd seen a glimpse of the devil. He turned and walked quickly for the door. I heard his laugh, high and cackling as he went down the corridor.

I put the gun down on the bed. My hands were shaking, the world was reverberating: it seemed like swarms of bees were flying back and forth between my ears. I tried to swallow some air and I remembered my sister's body laid out in the mortuary, my mother crying like a banshee.

I took the gun and went back to the bathroom. I pushed open the door. The tub had been drained and the room was empty. There was another door opposite. It led into another room identical to the first. There was a smell of something burning, and I found two cigarette butts smoldering in a triangular glass ashtray atop the bureau.

I heard some sirens wailing in a singsong pattern. I went to the window and drew the curtains. I pulled up the pane and saw a thin courtyard below. A narrow stone ledge ran along the building a few feet beneath me. I wiped the gun off as best I could with the hem of the curtain. I dropped it to the rug and kicked it beneath the bed. I was out the window and headed for the roof. The sound of the sirens grew louder and I thought I heard a distant crackling sound in the air.

I stood in Ladbrokes for a few hours betting the ponies. The little room was filled with cigarette smoke and the smell of wet raincoats. The floor was littered with pencil stubs and ripped-up wager tickets. Every once in a while I telephoned Parker, but no one answered.

In the third race at Nottingham, I bet a reverse forecast on Lupe's Joystick and Third Welkin, and won twenty-three quid after the tax. Then I lost a fiver on Rusting Angel in the fourth, and another seven betting each way on a deceitful mare named Gloria's Pudding in the sixth at Sedgefield.

I felt like walking out the door a winner. I put on my coat and ignored the yipping noises coming through the sound system, advancing notice of a late afternoon running of the dogs. Outside it was blowing wet snow and the stuff stuck in my eyelashes like runny glue.

I jumped aboard a bus headed for Tottenham Court Road. I went to the upper deck and sat down next to a woman holding a bag of turnips. I looked at the railings and the poles; there seemed to be a presence moving along the chrome, as if it were mercury and not metal.

At Piccadilly Circus there were protesters holding up placards in front of a church. We stopped for several minutes in the crush of the evening traffic and I tried to determine how one might live for others instead of for oneself, but I made little headway. Again I felt moons and meteors revolving around me, but now they were smaller, perhaps the size of plums and agate marbles, and soon enough it all retracted back inside my mind, and the bus began to move past the Trocadero.

I got off at Windmill Street and looked through the windows of the shops. The snow had stopped but the wind continued to blast across the pavement and up into my cuffs and sleeves. Inside a travel agency there was a poster of a bare-breasted woman eating a melon on a Caribbean beach. I pressed up against the glass and tried to count the goosebumps around her nipples, just to think of something else, just so no one would see me.

I made long strides for Goodge Street, taking the corner in front of the pub that was situated beneath Claudia's apartment. I walked inside to cadge a bit of their fire before going upstairs. I had a seat on a long padded bench before the fireplace and looked up at the reindeer's head that was mounted on the wall. Claudia and I had named him something once when we were very drunk, but I couldn't remember the name, only that Claudia kept spooning sugar into the brandy, and my teeth hurt when I drank it, and when I looked at her, I thought she was the Holy Prostitute of Christ Himself, and if I could just fuck her one more time they would have to nail me to a cross and the sins of the world would turn to clear water.

I walked out of the pub. Trenton Lee's blue limousine was parked at the curb. The chauffeur was leaning against the hood of a headlamp, smoking a cigarette. I went around the corner to the entrance of the apartment, and climbed the winding flight of stairs. I knocked four times on the door.

The peephole clicked open. The door went back a few inches; an unfamiliar nose appeared above the chain.

"Yes," said a high-pitched male voice.

"I want to see Claudia."

The nose withdrew. I heard some voices arguing from within. Finally the chain came off and Claudia was standing at the entrance with arms tightly folded, her fingertips touching her shoulders.

"What is it, Eddie?" she said curtly.

There was a cloud over her face; the corners of her lips were screwed down. Notwithstanding, she was famously dressed, wearing a short zebra-striped skirt, a clinging black silk blouse, and red alligator boots.

"I want to talk about love," I said.

"You'll have to hurry, then." She tapped her toe against the floorboard and coldly stared at me. "I've only a minute."

"You've got my keys. I can't get into my rooms."

"Oh right." She bit down on the edge of her lip. "Sorry."

"What's wrong?"

"Everything."

"Okay, then. Just give me my keys."

She hung her head and sighed. "It's Trenton's guitar player, Lyndon MacBeth. He's been picked up on Wardour Street for criminal possession. It's the second time in a fortnight. Trenton's lawyers are downtown trying to keep him from being thrown into choky. It's an awful mess."

"Well," I said. "I'll be out in a moment."

She took a small step, put her hands around my waist and her head on my shoulder, and began to cry. She was wearing a considerable dose of frangipani oil, and it was difficult to restrain myself from tearing off her blouse.

When she was through, she took a tissue from her pocket and meticulously dabbed at the corners of her eyes, so as not to smear her make-up. "Oh, come in for Christ's sake, Eddie!"

She led me through the atrium, around the corner and into the sitting room. It was dully lit with lamplight and a few scented candles. A haze of incense filled the air; motes of dust glimmered upon the surface of the oriental carpet. A long, lanky figure, obscured in the shadow, was lounging back on the divan.

"This is Eddie," said Claudia.

"Eddie?" said Trenton Lee, in a monotone. "I'm not supposed to know the wank, am I?"

"He's the one I'm married to."

"Well there's the pity." He sniffed loudly back through both nostrils and took a long drink from a bottle of champagne. "He doesn't mind that I've borrowed you, does he? I'm sure it won't be forever, chum."

My eyes began to adjust to the dim room. Trenton Lee was dressed in a blue leather suit, with starched white cuffs protruding beyond the sleeves of the jacket. He wore purple, iridescent boots with metal toecaps and spurs. I tried to make out his face, but his long dark hair was swept over his cheeks, so that only the inner corners of his eyes were exposed. The glint from one of the lamps showed a death's head tattooed in green ink on the back of his left hand; his fingers were covered with jewelry.

Claudia didn't answer right away. I could feel her smoldering, her barbed tongue caught in her mouth.

"Well," said Trenton Lee. "Does he want to have a look in me fuckin' pants, then? To see the awful weapon of record, what was used in the commission of the crime. Does he want me autograph, to shake me hand? It's all the same to me, really. I'm sitting and waiting for the telephone to ring." He took another drink of champagne, and softly belched.

"You're a rank asshole, Trenton," said Claudia.

"Better rank, than rank and file, love," he retorted. "Ricardo!"

A burly man, shaved bald in a three-piece suit scurried out of the bedroom. He flicked his hand against a switch on the wall and an overhead light went on. "What is it?" His domed head shifted slowly back and forth as he surveyed the room. "Go on, Trenton."

Trenton Lee pushed the hair from his eyes with his fingertips. His cheeks were heavily rouged and his face was eerily white. He rested his chin on his thumb and pouted his mouth.

"Search him."

"This is not necessary, Trenton!" exclaimed Claudia.

Trenton Lee leaned back in the divan.

The bodyguard approached and began going through my pockets. The top of his shaved head came barely up to my sternum. A black scorpion was tattooed in the middle of his scalp, and he wore a tiny hoop in his right ear. He thrust his arms under my coat and checked behind my back.

Trenton Lee looked on bemusedly. He lit an oval-shaped cigarette and placidly began smoking. Claudia took a seat on the other end of the divan and pretended to be perfectly at ease.

The bodyguard stuck his hand in my crotch. "Don't do that," I said. He ignored me. I dropped a glob of spit on his head.

He paid no attention and continued clapping his hands

down the sides of my legs, taking particular care with the boots. "He's clean, Trenton." He took a handkerchief from a pocket of his vest and wiped off the spittle.

"Do you think he's in with the law?"

"No—we've checked him out. He's got nothing to trade for."

"All right, then," said Trenton Lee. He produced a pair of yellow sunglasses with blue lenses and put them on. He took a long swallow of champagne and put his boots back on the table.

The telephone began to ring. Ricardo went to the kitchen and picked it up. Trenton Lee glared at me. "Doesn't he ever sit down, Claudia?"

Ricardo's head peeked around the arch that led into the kitchen. "It's Ridgeway, from the solicitors. The bail is set at a quarter million pounds."

Trenton Lee blinked his eyes and frowned. "My God," he said. "How much did they catch him with?"

"I don't know. What should I tell him?"

"What should you tell them! What should you fucking tell them!" A muscle in his face began to twitch. "It's they who are the bum-suckers with the little pissing bits of college paper, aren't they? Tell them to call the fucking accountants to release some funds from Lyndon's general account to pay the bail."

"There's not enough funds available in his account."

"What the devil are you talking about!" Trenton Lee jumped to his feet and threw his hands up in the air. "We just received a disbursement of three hundred thousand a piece for selling the concession rights on our Japanese tour."

"It's gone. There's only one hundred and seventy-five left."

"The asshole! The asshole!" He sat back down on the divan, took off his sunglasses and smashed them on the table. "He spent it on the dope." He rested his forehead against his palm, muttering.

"Hm, Let's see—so he's coming shy seventy-five thousand quid. How about that farm of his in Nottingham? Can't they take that in escrow? It must be worth at least a million. Christ, we have to play in Stockholm tomorrow night—they're writing a no-show clause now on Lyndon that would set us back half a million pounds. Yes—have them draw up a contract and let him sign over the farm. Those cocksuckers must know how to do something for all the money we pay them."

Ricardo shook his head. "It's one a.m. You can't hope to get started on something like that until the morning. The paperwork could take days."

Trenton Lee began scribbling on the table with an imaginary pencil. "Well you bloody don't expect *me* to put up the seventy-five grand, do you, Ricardo?" he said without looking up. "And turn down the goddamn lights. I feel like I'm sitting on the fucking sun.

"Okay, listen, Ricardo. Listen good. Tell them to call that wanking banker of ours, you know whatchamacallit Sir James fucking —"

"Hammersmith—"

"The right very bastard. Our Grand Cayman corporation must have about ten million pounds resting on its arsehole in his bank, accruing simple interest, or some such putrid thing. Yes, get a hold of him."

"It's one a.m."

"I *fucking* well *fucking* know it's one a.m., Ricardo. You already told me that. Just wake the bastard up. Drag—him—out—of his fucking bed. Leibowitz has power of attorney on that sort of thing. Yes. Wake up Leibowitz too, and his dogs, and his whole fucking family. Tell him to meet Sir fucking Hammersmith at the bank."

Ricardo nodded. He blinked a few times. "I'll try to do that," he said.

"Good."

The bodyguard disappeared around the archway. Trenton Lee picked at his hair for a few moments, then lit another cigarette. "Good God," he said, "that heroin is nasty stuff. Have the P.R. people been notified, Claudia?"

"I called them."

"Do you think they can fabricate the quotations on their own, or do I have to go and hold their dicks for them too?" He blew a jet of smoke at the ceiling and played with one of the huge diamond rings that larded his fingers. "Oh fuck—I can't do everything. We must go now. They'll be after me to co-sign that loan. How about that new club in Knightsbridge you were boasting about?"

"I have to change."

"No time for that." Trenton Lee dropped his cigarette into a half-filled champagne glass, then looked at me menacingly. "Will you be coming with us—uh, Eddie, is it? I have a change of clothes in the closet that you could borrow."

"Some other time."

"Trenton, you're horrid," said Claudia.

"I know. They pay me for it ... Ricardo! Have you finished?"

"Yes," came a shrill, lilting voice. "It's done."

"Do we have a sell order out if Royal Dutch Petroleum goes above ninety?"

"Yes."

"What about those animal ... belly futures on the Chicago market?"

Ricardo's balloon-shaped head appeared at the rim of the arch. He had an orange and white dish towel in his hand and was wiping clean a china plate. "There's some sort of scare over there," he said.

"Oh, right, oh right. A swine disease in sheep-fucking Iowa. It's obvious bullshit, but it will push up the prices, won't it. Good. Let's sit on it. Are you ready, sweetness?"

Claudia packed up her make-up kit. She gave her hair twenty rapid strokes of the brush, stood up and came over to me. She got down on one knee and put her head on my lap.

"Everything's all right, isn't it Eddie?" she said softly. "We don't mind all this, do we?"

"No, we don't," I answered.

Trenton Lee was standing by the window looking out on Goodge Street. He pulled back the curtain and pressed his pallid face to the glass. His skin reflected blue and red and he began humming a tune in a minor key.

"It would be inconvenient for me to go to London Bridge now," I said. "I'm going to sleep on your couch again."

"Of course," said Claudia. She rose to her feet and suddenly grabbed me around the neck with her hands and began to squeeze. "But stay out of my lingerie drawer, and don't steal anything."

"Yes," assented Trenton Lee, turning from the window. "Otherwise we shall have you shot. Isn't that so, Ricardo?"

Ricardo appeared behind me, headed for the door. He wore a trilby hat and an overcoat. "Yes," he said. He pulled a revolver from his pocket and opened up the door. He looked back and forth in the hallway, then spun around to face us. "That's right," he said. "Come on, Trenton, Wilson has the car ready."

I dreamed that a black dog with a long glassy snout had my neck in his jaws. The snout turned into a clear cylinder and it was filled with my blood.

I woke up in Claudia's bed. I groped for the clock on the nightstand and held it up to my face. The phosphorescent hands glowed barely five-thirty. My mind filled with black thoughts.

I put on my spectacles and hobbled through the dark into the bathroom.

I flicked on the lamp. The walls had been repainted in rose and ultramarine; the tones were blinding. I scrabbled through the medicine chest; it was half-filled with men's toiletries of curious label and scent. I tried to locate Claudia's bottle of morphine tablets, but it was too well-hidden. I read the label inside a bright red brassiere.

I went into the parlor and took from the bookcase a volume about surrealism. I sat on the sofa and leafed through the color plates. The splintered images, bloated protoplasm, and lucid depictions of things not right, mirrored well my own thoughts.

I stood up and looked through the window over Goodge Street. Several police cars were parked on either side of the roadway. I opened the window a few inches. A blue light was spinning and the bizarre crackle of two-way radios split the air.

I took up the field glasses and had a closer look. In one of the cars, a screw-faced nit from special forces was cleaning an assault rifle with a pale cloth. Another officer tossed a cigarette end from the window; it landed on the pavement sparking like fireflies.

Several weeks went by. Every Sunday I went to the Portobello Road to sell bric-a-brac to the passers-by. During the week I traveled the rounds of dusty out-of-the-way shops in search of merchandise. When the ledger sheets didn't add up, I shoplifted and stole to balance out the columns. It wasn't a very noble existence, but it suited me as well as the next thing.

It happened one morning that I woke up in my apartment and began to think of Claudia. It was unusual that she wouldn't call me for such a long stretch of time, if for no other reason than to harass me. I rang her up, but there was no answer.

I hadn't been outside for three or four days. Sometimes I'd go downstairs and look out through the glass of the front door, but I got no further. I thought of going to the National Gallery and looking at a Van Eyck. We must make God a man in order to paint his image. That was the essence of Christianity.

I sat down on the horsehair sofa and drank a cup of coffee. I looked through a pornographic magazine and read some essays of De Quincey. I turned on the radio and rolled the dial until I found some tonal jazz.

The telephone exploded. I let it ring fifteen times before I picked it up.

"Hello."

"Eddie."

I carried the handset over to the window and peered out. Some youths were playing soccer in the street. They had on tattered coats and wore no hats. When a car came along, they'd barely move aside to let it pass.

"Eddie."

"Yes."

"It's Claudia."

"I know," I said. "I've been thinking about you." But really I was thinking that Schubert died when he was thirty-one.

"There's a woman here at the apartment. She claims she knows you."

"What's her name?"

"She never said ..."

The sky was gray and bleak. A pale bird—the color of winter—flew past the window and landed on an eave. The soccer ball took a bounce on the roof of a car, and fell into a hedge.

"What's she look like?"

"Rather cheap ... rather expensive," said Claudia. "Such as you would fancy."

There was Art Tatum on the piano, but I kept thinking about Schubert, thirty-one, Mozart, thirty-five, Keats, twenty-six. I looked at the spot on my wrist where I used to wear a watch.

"What are you talking about?"

"She's quite amusing, isn't she? Fashion, music, violence, Buñuel."

"Can she hear you?"

"I'm in the kitchen," said Claudia. "Have you been in her pants?"

"What is it?"

"She wants to see you."

"Yes."

I put down the receiver. The jazz stopped and the news came on. The announcer's voice was soft, but clarion. A bomb in the Frankfurt airport. Two boys fought for the ball; the brakes of a dull green lorry screeched.

I found my coat and went downstairs. I looked through my mail. A letter from my father; a circular from the supermarket. I dropped them in the dustbin, unopened.

As I walked out the door the soccer ball came flying at my face. I thrust out my hands to catch it, but it hit my wrist and spun away.

"Dickface!"

I walked down the street towards London Bridge. At Crosby Row I stopped before the window of a butcher's shop to remove a mote of dust from my eye. Small pigs, smoked pink, with hooves removed, hung from ropes.

I crossed the bridge on foot. A tyranny of traffic surrounded me. A thin man with gray goggles sped by on a motorcycle. A strap snapped on the back of the bike, and a cargo of boxes went flying off. They exploded open on the pavement and a thousand pieces of paper went flying.

A busker was playing a twelve-string guitar at Bank Station. The instrument had a fine tinny ring, and he sang an old Donovan number in a high tenor. He wore a funny little cloth cap, and his hair was long and dirty. The notes wavered, echoing through the passage, and I could see that everyone wanted to stop for a second and take hold of an unearthly moment.

I daydreamed and missed my stop. I got off at Oxford Circus and walked up the end of Regent Street. In the windows of the shops I saw canopies raised over bathtubs, Union Jack underwear, toy erector sets, ghastly mannequins and fashions. Cans of green and orange tomato paste flanked sinuous perfume bottles. There was a sign for West End blood donors.

I turned right at Mortimer Street and passed the hospital. Some old bums were screaming in front of a scaffolding. I stopped and listened to them for a few minutes, and everything they said was truth.

I waited a long while at Claudia's door. Finally, Ricardo

pulled back the chain.

"What is it, friend?" he drawled. There was a bleary look in his eyes, and one of his shirttails had nearly worked its way loose from his trousers.

"I've come to see Claudia."

"I've not been told of it," he said.

"This is my flat," I countered. "The lease is in my name."

He winked at me and smiled expansively. He took a few short breaths. "So it is, friend," he said. "The Indians own North America for that matter. But what's a piece of paper worth when you're faced with superior firepower?" He patted at something beneath his waistcoat.

"It's seven years in the dock if they catch you with that thing."

He bit on a fingernail, his eyes gleaming. I looked at his pupils; they were small as pinpricks. "That's only if they catch me alive—dead men don't serve time, friend." The smile disappeared.

"Let me in."

He pursed his lips, his throat tightened. The color drained from his face. He appeared to be getting sick. He shook his head, trying to gain purchase of himself. "There's a flashy Dutch cunt been here—says she's looking for you."

I stared at him blankly.

"Platinum hair, black leather, funny accent," he continued. "You wouldn't soon forget her. Makes you want to chain yourself to the wall ... you know what I mean?"

I nodded. "Sure."

He grabbed me by the arm and looked at me beseechingly. His breath smelled of peppermint. "How do you come by these fancy quiffs, friend? That Claudia—she'd give a stiff a hard-on ... Trenton, I understand. He buys 'em, trades 'em for a touch of his fame. But ..." he searched for the words, "you ain't got a leg on to nothing—do you? You're zero. Ain't you?"

I shrugged my shoulders. "It's not divided up that way,"

I said. "Not all the time, at least. Why don't you give me a taste of what you've got, okay."

He looked at me bug-eyed and started giggling. He squeezed on my arm. "You don't give a shit, do you friend?"

"It's too late for all that," I said.

He took a green glass vial from his waistcoat pocket and carefully screwed off the top. He jabbed in his finger and lifted up a mound of violet-stained powder, held it to his left nostril and sucked it up. He repeated the motion, offering me the fingertip.

"What's the purple stuff?"

"I believe it's cut with a wee bit of magic, mate. To give it body."

We stood there in the doorway waiting. There was music playing in the apartment, arpeggios on a synthesizer, an amplified viola; it was tinny and muffled. I began to taste bitter phlegm in my throat, there seemed to be something coming up from behind my nose into my eyeballs and pharynx.

Ricardo led me into the parlor. Jana and Claudia were sprawled out on the rug playing cards. There were neat stacks of poker chips at their elbows, and cigarettes burning in china ashtrays. A nearly empty half liter of Spanish brandy stood between them.

Jana's silver hair was filled with flowers; a lynx coat was wrapped around her shoulders. She threw down the nine of hearts and took a sip from a turquoise noggin.

"Is that you, Eddie?" she said without looking up.

Claudia slipped a card from the top of the deck and slid it across the carpet. She tugged at the pearls that hung from her neck and rubbed her bare feet together. She expelled the knave of clubs and the six of diamonds and picked up two cards to replace them.

"Hello, darling," she said. "You don't mind if your women decide your fate over a game of cards?"

"Oh," I replied, sounding disappointed. "I thought you were playing for money."

"We play poker for love," said Jana, picking up her fill card. "Everything else we play for money." She surveyed her hand and studied Claudia's face. She pushed a blue chip into the kitty. "Five pounds."

"You're lying, Jana," I said.

"All the girls lie to you, Eddie," said Claudia. "Match you and raise it five." She flipped over two blue chips and took a draw on a cigarette.

I looked at the Morris chair next to the bookcase. Its legs seemed rubbery; the wood expanded and contracted. A spectrum of microscopic lights glittered in the whorling patterns of the carpet. My lungs felt like dried ice and it seemed that the blood was running through my veins at double speed.

"How come you leave without saying goodbye to Jana? You are not a very nice boy, Eddie ..." Jana stared at the backs of Claudia's cards. She took another sip from the noggin and passed her fingers over her fanned-out hand. "I see you and go five once more."

Claudia chewed on her pearls. She was wearing a thin angora sweater, the neckline plunging, her breasts swelling out. I wanted to drop to the floor and roll over like a dog.

"Why are you saying such awful things about my husband, Jana?" she asked. She looked up suddenly. Jana didn't bat an eyelash. Claudia spread her cards on the floor. She held three sixes, a queen and a deuce.

"He's mine now," said Jana. She turned her head slightly and smiled. She lay her cards down one at a time: a diamond flush, knave high.

Claudia pushed over the deck in disgust. She took a drag on her cigarette and sputtered smoke in Jana's face. "You're cheating, you bitch," she said sharply.

Jana pulled in the chips in the kitty and stacked them neatly on top of her own pile. She flapped her hand at the wrist to dissipate the smoke. "Of course I am cheating. We are playing rules of the house, I thought."

She smiled again. Her face looked like the sun; coronas

and nimbuses revolved about her head, and I thought that if I jumped at her I would dissolve and flow inside her roseate skin.

Claudia started giggling. She took a draught from Jana's mug and sprayed a fine mist of liquid in the air. "If you have poison for me—I will drink it," she pronounced gravely. "I love you, Jana. Please stay and play cards with me forever."

I excused myself and went into the kitchen. Ricardo was sitting at the table reading a blueprint. He seemed to have sprouted two bumps above his forehead; his skin was crawling with small circumrotatory organisms.

"What's that?" I asked.

He shook his head and looked up at me. He looped his ring finger through the ear-shaped handle of a flowered teacup, and raised it to his lips. "It's the floor plan of a concert hall in Kyoto. We're playing there again in May. I've had the Japanese police forward it to me." He took a sip of the tea and slashed at the paper with a blue pencil.

"Security?"

"T-shirt sales."

I went to the cupboard above the sink and took down a pint of Canadian whiskey. I poured a pony into a shot glass and batted it down. I did it twice again. I studied the row of orchids beneath a green glass shade on a shelf over the counter. Pins pricked me in the eyes and my fingers were long and elastic.

I drank some more, standing up. I watched the glow of the fluorescent light on the black flowers. I heard the scratching of the pencil on the blueprints and the clinking of the teacup against the saucer.

I woke up on the floor of the bedroom. It was dark outside. There were voices coming from the bathroom, then a tinkling of glass. The world seemed like it was pulling backwards, as if it would be sucked up through my eyeballs before disappearing ...

The door to the bathroom opened splashing a horrible light in my face. Lyndon MacBeth walked out; he was a giant. He ducked his head to avoid the lintel, and nearly stumbled on his feet. His massive shoulders were girded by a velvet cape, in his hands he held a cylindrical fur-covered hat.

"Come girls," he said in an effeminate tone. He positioned the hat on his head, and then pulled down on the baggy skin beneath his eyes. "Girls!" he screamed.

Two very young girls, sixteen, perhaps, with strawberry blonde hair, followed him into the room. They both wore little black miniskirts and white silk blouses, with three or four ermine stoles wrapped about their arms and necks. They had on black skullcaps hung with veils and teetered about on high-heeled shoes.

"So is that it then, girls?" inquired Lyndon MacBeth. "The last drop?"

"Yes," said one of them. "I promise, Lyndon."

"Don't promise me. Promises break my heart. You'll just have to go home now." He raised his voice: "That's right! Into the street."

"Goddamn it, Lyndon," said the other one, in a grating American voice. "Calm down already. We still got some more shit—Tuesday hid it in her shoe."

The first girl bent over and pulled off one of her pumps. She beat the side of it against her palm and a plastic bag popped out. Quick as a fly, MacBeth grabbed it from her and began pulling at the plastic with his long nimble fingers. "What is it! What is it, April!" he cried.

The girl April grabbed at his wrist and bit into the skin below the knuckles. "Ouch!" he yelled. He batted her against the cheek and she went flying back into the arms of her associate.

"It's strychnine," said April, steadying herself against her friend. "I hope you fucking die, Lyndon, you maniac."

I closed my eyes and disappeared. When I came to, Lyndon MacBeth was standing against the wall with his trousers lowered past his knees. The women were performing fellatio on him. The whiskey had worn off, but not the drug, and their bodies and the wall seemed to be moving together, as if we were aboard a rocking ship.

I crawled into the bathroom to attempt recovery. There were framed photographs on the wall: Olivier in *Lear*, Paul Robeson in *Othello*. The cover of a record album was lying on the rug. Trenton Lee was looking into a crystal ball that contained the cadaverous faces of the remainder of the band. A gray cross was tattooed onto Lyndon MacBeth's forehead.

I pulled myself up and filled the basin with freezing water from the tap. I removed my spectacles and stuck my face in it while I counted ninety. I emerged and looked into the mirror. The world was still squirting backwards through my eye sockets. The image in the glass nearly lifted off; everything was thin dust and vapor. A bottle of crême de cassis was sitting in the shower. I drank from it until there was some stabilization of matter.

In the parlor the lights were dimmed and the air smelled of fragrant oils. There were trays of meats and cheeses on the lowboys, white bottles of beer and thin crystal flutes.

Trenton Lee was sitting on the sofa punching numbers into a gold-plated calculator. He was wearing a swallow-tail coat and a top hat; his hair was pulled back in a pony-tail and he had on tortoise shell sunglasses.

"Did you check out those two little sluts that Lyndon brought in, Ricardo?" he said. He transcribed a sum into a small, leather-bound notebook.

The bodyguard issued forth from the shadows. He held a two-way radio in one hand and one of his ears was bandaged. "There's nothing more to them. I found some more dope secreted in their coats. It's down the kitchen drain."

"Heroin?"

"Yes, but tossed up with something else. It's lavender. LSD perhaps. We fed some to the cat." He winked at me.

Trenton Lee groaned. "We'll have to get him back in the detox after we do that photo session in Rimini. Can he make it until Tuesday?"

"I don't know, Trenton. Perhaps not."

"What happened to that doctor we had in Luxembourg? We could bring him along for a few days."

"He's doing five to ten," said Ricardo.

"Pity that," said Trenton Lee. "He played a good game of whist. Is there any of that morphine base cough syrup left?"

"Hydrocodone bitartrate."

"Yes, whatever." He put his feet up on the coffee table. His boots were crusted with emeralds. "Feed him a few tablespoons twice a day—keep him absolutely in handcuffs! We're debited half a million pounds if he no-shows tomorrow in Milan. I've told you and told you ... It's in the contract now, after the fiasco on the Isle of Wight ... Then back to the farm at Lausanne—hang him on the clothesline."

Ricardo slipped a pocket watch from his vest pocket and contemplated it. "Why do you keep him, Trenton? He's a total liability."

With a fingertip, the rock star trawled the letter z through the condensation on a flasket of beer. "Why, indeed," he said contemplatively. "I'll tell you why—" he wagged his thumb in the air. "Because he's a musical genius. He can play the violin like Heifetz, and slide guitar like bleeding Elmore James himself. He can transcribe from memory the score of every pop tune ever written, and he can harmonize like the son of God against my wretched voice ... And he's a star—pure star. Little boys love him, little girls love him—me own mum loves him. Do you remember my solo album, Ricardo? It would be strange—because no one else does ... No thanks. He's a junkie and a pimp, but he's my junkie, my pimp. I'm the golden egg, but he's the goose ...

"Bah, enough of this chatter." He fixed the stay of a diamond cuff link and sneered at the flasket. "Now quickly, Ricardo. What about this convertible bond offering at United British Airwaves? Is it a set-up? Or what, then? I'm ready to go in with a hundred thousand pounds sterling."

The bodyguard pointed his chin at me.

"Oh come, now," said Trenton Lee. "He's nothing to worry about. We've put him in charge of procuring women and freeloading." He closed his eyes in concentration. "Tell me—what's the pound at against the dollar?"

"A pound will buy you two dollars-forty." said Ricardo.

"It's soaring."

"Seems like it."

Trenton Lee rubbed his hands together. He removed his sunglasses and rolled his eyes up. "What's our boy in Whitehall say?"

"Come again?"

"Oh—don't be coy with me, Ricardo. I really haven't the time." The rock star excised a rasher of prosciutto from a cold meat tray and dangled it before his mouth, then dropped it in.

"You know," he continued, squinting at a lamp, "Lord Quiffquaff, or whatever you call him."

"Can't be bought anymore."

"Of course he can. Have you tried getting him properly laid?"

Ricardo shook his head. A dapple of blood had soaked through the bandage on his ear. "Don't believe he's heterosexually inclined."

"Well then you fuck him, mate."

"Anything else?'

"Lots of things," replied the rock star. "The days are short, and my greed is endless. Take a few pounds from our account in Basel and buy two hundred thousand dollars. Place a sell order back into pounds when it drops to two bucks."

"If the pound drops. What if it goes up?"

"Damn me forever if that will happen," said Trenton Lee. "With Reagan in there to shill? They'll decontrol the moon ..."

He agitated his forehead with his ring and middle finger and exhaled deeply. "Why are the police still breathing down our collars?"

A puzzled look crossed Ricardo's face. He returned his pocket watch to the waistcoat and touched his bandage. "They say there's a syndicate from the continent trying to float a whopping wad of heroin into London. If you wanted to sell half kilos at retail prices, where would you go?"

Trenton Lee nodded his head. He tapped the crown of a pencil against a thumbnail. "Our boy Lyndon. Keep an eye on him, Ricardo, or it's back to the sewer with you—where I found you."

"It wasn't noticeably different from here," said Ricardo, retiring back into the shadows.

I walked into the vestibule. I studied the design of the new wallpaper: colored rhomboids swirling against the grain, emerald green on purple, lapidary, endless.

Someone grabbed my hand. Hot breath flushed against my ear. "You made my heart empty when you are gone, Eddie," whispered Jana. "I didn't know it at first, some days pass. Then another day ... when the sun wakes me up ... I am crying ... my soul is hollow ... I didn't understand. Even my blackness had some light before ... but it left with you."

"You're piss-drunk, Jana," I said.

She put her arm around my waist and put her hand against my cheek. "What of that? The drunk ones cannot love? One fire cannot light the other? The moment may come at any time—asleep, awake, drunk or nearly dead ..."

She felt like magic, a gift of the northern God—who cared what was underneath? I closed my eyes and pulled her face to mine. Through the liquor, the lysergic acid ascended again, fabricated words echoed in the inner ear, a red diamond. I walked down a long hall, Mantegna's *Death of Mary*, the paint falling from the canvas in Madrid, haloes above the deathbed, the mother dies in us all ...

I opened my eyes and looked at Jana through my clouded lenses. Her cheeks were wet, I didn't know with whose tears.

"Come, Eddie, I am happy now," she said smiling. Her nose was pierced with a ruby, it burst in my sight like a shooting star. "Do you like these music people? I do, so much ... My grandfather played the piano before the crowd in Budapest—do you know? He left the earth when I was a little girl. I am carrying him in my memory always. He plays for me in my dreams. He wears a long black coat, a fish the color of roses is lying on the piano..."

There was shouting in the parlor. Down the corridor, Lyndon MacBeth, hair disheveled and great face glowing like a tungsten lamp, had entered and grabbed Ricardo by the collar.

Jana took my wrist, drawing us into the room. The smaller man was raining ineffectual blows at the chest of the towering guitarist. He went for his gun. Lyndon MacBeth swatted it away and pinned Ricardo's wrists to the wall.

"By the bones of Christ, Ricardo!" he shouted. "What are you doing to me! Tell me what!" MacBeth's face turned purple, his eyes popped like a toad's. He grabbed the bodyguard by the neck. Trenton Lee jumped from the sofa and ran up to them. "Easy now, Lyndon. Good God— what is this." He latched onto MacBeth's forearm, and tried to turn the wrist.

"He's destroyed all the drugs!" wailed Lyndon MacBeth.

"What!"

"The drugs. He's taken them all and flushed them down the jakes ... Aargh! Aargh!" The giant guitarist began groaning like he was in the throes of death. "As if they were common and lowly as he!"

He let go of Ricardo's neck and shoved away Trenton Lee. "By Christ, I'm going to throw you through the window, Ricardo!" He clutched at the bodyguard and began dragging him by the arm across the floor. "You fucking traitor. You fucking Judas!"

Trenton Lee walked alongside them waving his arms.

"Let go, Lyndon!" he implored. "You'll destroy us all. You're mad. You're out of choky on two-hundred grand bail, remember? If they catch you with as much as an aspirin, they'll fry your English balls in butter!"

"I don't care," exploded Lyndon MacBeth, "I don't fucking care!" He gritted his teeth and violently shook his head ... He threw Ricardo to the ground and began jumping up and down causing all the furniture to tremble.

"I need me drugs!" he screamed. "I need me drugs!"

He began pounding wildly on the bookcase. Some plates were stacked on one of the shelves; they dislocated and flew to the floor shattering. He picked up a Ching vase and hurled it at the wall.

"I need them! I need them!"

Jana loosened my wrist and took a step forward. "Lyndon! Lyndon! You must stop this ... Isn't life hell enough without hurting the others?"

MacBeth looked at her in disbelief. He seemed paralyzed; his eyes were frozen open.

Jana stepped closer to him. "You must make quiet in your head now, Lyndon. You must—or you are lost."

MacBeth leaned against the bookcase and collapsed to the floor. He dropped his face into his hands. His chest heaved, his breaths came short and fast.

"Quiet, quiet, Lyndon," said Jana. She softly touched a spot in the middle of his forehead. She bent over and whispered something in his ear.

"Come on now." She stroked his arm, like a cat. "We will take a little walk along the street. The cold air will wash you off."

Lyndon MacBeth hugged himself and briefly shivered. He pushed his hands against his temples, and began to rise from the floor. Jana buttoned her coat at the neck.

"Go with them, Ricardo," said Trenton Lee.

The bodyguard pretended to wipe dust from his suit. "I'd sooner take a bullet through me bean," he said.

Jana unplaited one of her braids and let the lock hang loose on her cheekbone. Her eyes were burning, but her face was cold as frost.

"He is in a bad time," she said in a clear voice. "You can drop the money on his head until he falls through the ground ..."

"We don't want to be no John Lennon," shot back Trenton Lee. "Call someone else up from security, Ricardo. Get a move on." He gave Jana an ugly glare. "Sorry girlie."

"Don't be afraid of yourself, Lyndon. That is the only danger." She pulled on her gloves and raised her hand to the guitarist. "Only from ourselves. It is always like that." She turned to me, her face filled with resolve. "I am going now. Shall you come with me, Eddie?"

"No, no!" cried Lyndon MacBeth. "She's the truth, Trenton." He stood up to his full height and locked his hands together.

"And I'm a lie, I suppose," said Trenton Lee.

MacBeth walked over to the window and pulled up the glass. The lights from Goodge Street smeared across his forehead. He raised one of his purple boots and placed it on the ledge. "I go with her, or I go out the window. That's all," he said calmly. "That's the end."

Trenton Lee held up his fingernails. They were painted black and adorned with silver stars. He looked at them closely, biting down on his lip. "Oh go fuck yourselves, all of you. We're screwed either way." He slapped his palms down on the coffee table. "Go ahead you sorry bastards. We'll just have to play with whatever wretched hand we're dealt ... Return his carcass by six a.m. though, would you, darling? We have a plane to catch to Italy ...Give her a hundred quid, Ricardo ... Get a receipt—"

A minute later I stood at the window and watched them standing beneath a street lamp at the curb. An ice cream moon hung in the winter sky. A taxi pulled up and they disappeared inside it, Jana following Lyndon MacBeth.

One of the two young girls stumbled in from the bedroom. She was wearing only pumps and panties; her make-up was streaked across her face. She caught her balance, then tottered again on her heels. She grabbed at a lamp with a paisley shade, sending it tumbling to the floor.

"Trenton," she said hoarsely.

Trenton Lee looked up from his drink. "Oh—what is it now, April?"

"I think Tuesday's dead."

"Do I look like the fucking coroner?'

The girl's eyelids flickered and her head dipped down. She braced her palms against the wall and tried to make her way along it.

"Trenton," she said, her voice hoarse and dry.

"Yes."

"Tuesday's dead, I said."

I went outside. The ice cream moon was clear and free of clouds; in an empty plain or forest, one might even be guided by its light. But in great London, the street lamps lorded over the moon and stars, and worlds of stone and wheels of rubber had sprung up in geometric madness, as if from dragons' teeth planted in the ground.

It was nearly dawn when I reached my apartment. I looked to the east; a layer of orange slowly suffused the blackness of night, punctured by the diamond eye of Venus.

I climbed three stairs and sat down on the stoop. I was winded and swept through with vertigo after the long night. The air was clear and chilly; I raised the collar of my coat so that it covered my neck. I drew the coldness back through my nostrils and it flooded my brain; I breathed heavily out through my mouth. In the first light of dawn, all forms began changing: gates and shrubs, the base of a lamppost, the drawn curtains in the windows across the street.

A milk truck rolled down the pavement; the noise was deafening. I held my hand to my throat. It felt hot and pulsating. I swallowed; the Adam's apple thrust against my palm.

I started thinking about Jana, and then I couldn't stop. She appeared, disappeared, in a kaleidoscope of faces. My sister lacing up her dance shoes, the ghastly white features of Mary at the cross, Miss America walking down the runway in Atlantic City. I shook my head until the images were gone, until I was left with a deep hollow.

I went up to my rooms and lay down on the horsehair couch. It had turned morning and the winter light forced itself stiffly through the curtains, spotting the walls. I closed my eyes to keep it out, but it pierced my eyelids and traveled down to the center of my mind.

There was a soft knocking on the door. I stayed where I was, shutting my eyes tighter. It started again, softer still, distant, rhythmically thudding. I drifted into sleep. I was in a motel in New Mexico, pastel, strange light, climbing the stairs. On the patio, floors above, I looked over the rail at the swimming pool. The knocking was loud and hammering.

"What is it?"

"Let me in." The voice was muffled through the wood. "I must talk to you."

"Okay, just a minute."

I started counting the spots on the ceiling. It was quiet for a long while. I can decide not to decide I thought. I closed my eyes; I felt adrift in a rowboat in a great sea. The hand across the water. With great concentration I controlled my gag reflex. Something smashed against the door ... it flew open, splintering, and banged against the wall.

I opened my eyes. Werner was standing over me, staring down at my face. A black fedora was tipped back on his head exposing the forehead and a shock of hair. His green eyes were water. In one of his hands he held a cigar, unlit. He brushed something from the collar of his greatcoat.

"Where is Jana?" he asked.

"I don't know."

He pulled me from the couch to the floor and kicked me in the ribs. I held my hands against my side.

"You don't think I am playing a game, do you, Eddie?" He kicked me again, precisely, viciously, with the point of his boot.

I probed my ribs with the tips of my fingers, and tried to take a breath. The back of my neck felt like it was stuck through with needles. "No. It's not a game," I said with difficulty, my voice choked.

"Where is Jana?'

"It doesn't matter," I said.

"What!" He rolled the cigar nervously between his thumb and middle finger. I could smell the scented tobacco leaves.

"It's too late." My tongue was parched.

"What are you talking about—you asshole." He leaned over and grabbed me by the collar. He raised my torso up a few inches and began shaking me violently, then slammed me back against the floor.

"Is this what you mean?" he said. He raised me up a few inches, then did it again. The room was shaking.

"Hey! Come in," he cried.

Into the room walked Ralph. His hair was greased back with oil and a worsted wool suit fit him poorly. My vision went double and for a moment there were two of him. He wore black Clark Kent glasses, and had his hands clasped behind his back. Between his legs I could see the fat end of a cricket bat.

"Mornin' mate," he said. "Have you come down with a touch of the grippe then—all laid out on your back, like a turtle getting ready for the soup." He peered down over his pitted nose. His skin was blanched and his eyes were dead.

"Hold him down," commanded Werner.

Ralph leered at me; a smile formed on his bluish lips. "Can't I just wallop the God-holy shit out of him first? It would be a pleasure meet." He brought out one of his hands and showed an empty palm. Then he swung out the other, choking the bat mid-stick. "Just a few gentle blows to the head."

"Time for that later," said Werner. "Do you have some of that rum?"

Ralph rested the tip of the bat on the floor and reached into his pocket. "Got it here in my jacket. Half of the half-pint ... But I'm damned to hell if I hold the little bastard to. Just don't move, son." He took out a small bottle with a butterfly on the label and began to unscrew the cap. "Or else I'll bust your face up like a rotten jack-o'-lantern."

Werner produced a vinyl case from inside his coat. He unfolded it, revealing a row of syringes secured by elastic bands. He extracted one and turned it to and fro.

He dipped the needle in the neck of the rum bottle and delicately pulled back the plunger. Ralph's hand began to shake.

"Hold it still, you fool."

The sun had come up above the level of the windows, and the room was flooded with daylight. I could see all the bones beneath their skulls. The cloth of the window curtains was frayed and shining.

"Make your fist in a ball."

"I'm sure you'll like it, mate. We call it a cheap trip to Jamaica."

I grabbed the deltoid of my left arm and clenched my fist. The needle slid into my vein. Werner pulled back slightly to get a register of blood, then pushed down quickly on the plunger. A slug of fire shot up my arm and out through the top of my head. My ears rang like church bells.

"Where is Jana?"

"She went with Lyndon MacBeth." The world smelled like an ocean of burning sugar. I thought my brain would explode.

Werner swore in Swiss-German. Ralph prodded me in the stomach with the cricket bat. "Lie still, mate," he cautioned. "There's a tempest going to blow through the islands."

"Shut up!" said Werner. He clutched his forehead in the span of his fingers, and clenched his teeth. "I should have strangled that gypsy cunt in Edinburgh." He pushed down on my nose with his index finger. "Eddie. Do you see what she has done."

"Yes." The rush of the rum began to abate and I knew I wouldn't die. I pushed away the finger.

"She stole the weight from me—yes." He jabbed me in the eye. "She's going to sell it to the world's richest junkie ... rock and roll swine ... one-trick pony."

He sat down next to my feet, agitating his cheeks with his palms. "What am I going to do? ... Where is MacBeth now?"

"Milan."

"Fuck ... There is a heavy price on my head there ... No, I'll have to go out and find that gypsy ... and kill her ... Nothing else will do."

"Gypsy?'

"Yes," said Werner, hanging on the word. He took out a green silk handkerchief and spotted his face. "You don't know. Jana is Swiss gypsy. Romansh. A few are left the Nazis did not kill."

Ralph pushed the bat into my kidney. I grabbed the end of it. "Let it be, mate! I have to make gray mush of your brain." He tugged back at it viciously. I sat up and let go of my end, sending him tumbling.

Ralph started laughing maniacally. I got up off the couch and went to the window. I raised it a few inches to take the air. My vision was crawling with spots and lines. The window was barred; I pushed my face against the cold metal. A woman passed by pushing a perambulator.

"Stay away from there," called Werner. I turned around.

"Let me have a geeze, your honor," said Ralph to Werner. "It will bring us luck."

Werner handed him the vinyl case. "Use the one with a black dot on it."

Ralph extracted one of the remaining syringes and sat

down on the arm of the couch. He removed half his jacket and carefully rolled up his sleeve.

The barrel of the syringe was already half filled with liquid. Ralph held it up; the needle gleamed like an ancient eye. He slid it deftly into a vein on the back of his hand.

Ralph looked at Werner, a daft smile turning the corners of his mouth. "What's the nature of my treat?" He pulled back the plunger. A jet of blood registered in the barrel.

"Part heroin, part cocaine," said Werner. He returned the vinyl case to his pocket. Ralph smoothly pushed down the plunger, injecting the reddened solution.

"And part surprise."

"I like surprises."

Ralph's eyes and mouth opened wide. He gasped and jerked his arms back over his shoulders, rising to his full height. The syringe flopped against his arm and he keeled forward, landing flat on his face crashing onto the floor.

Werner adjusted the brim of the fedora and buttoned up his overcoat. "That's a pity about that," he said. "Sometimes ... but only sometimes ... science is unreliable." He walked to the door, opened it and walked out. "If you see her first, Eddie ... send Jana my love."

Blood seeped out from Ralph's nose. I put my hand beneath his chin and turned his head. The cartilage was twisted, the nose broken by the fall. A lens had popped from his spectacles.

I took the syringe into the bathroom and threw it in the commode. I watched the explosion of water as I pulled the overhead chain. The syringe didn't go down; it bobbed in the water like a fishing lure. I pulled the chain once more and it disappeared.

I went back and looked at Ralph. All you could see was the twisted nose. I rolled up his sleeve and buttoned it at the cuff. I called a taxi.

I went through his pockets. I found fifty pounds, and the business card of a hotel in Swiss Cottage.

The cab driver had a birdlike face, small eyes and spavine nose. He cleared his throat and held his hand in a fist a few inches forward of his mouth, as if he was holding a microphone.

"Called a taxi?"

"There's a man here, I don't know him—he's very drunk. Can you take him to his hotel?"

"I suppose." He tried to look over my shoulder.

I gave him the fifty quid. He looked at it momentarily and stuffed it into his pocket. He pushed his way around me and walked toward Ralph. He grabbed him under the arms, went down on one knee, and hauled him up, locking one of Ralph's arms around his neck.

"Should I help."

"No sir—it's in my hands now."

I closed the door behind them and started drinking a pint of Old Granddad. It was nearly noon and the apartment was filled with sunlight.

The sun was out again the next day. I went down to the corner store and bought a bunch of newspapers. I lugged them back to the apartment, fried an egg and brewed a cup of coffee. I washed a fork and plate and sat down at the table.

I read the finance pages. Reagan and Thatcher were going to send the stock markets roaring up into space. Pictures of them smiling ear to ear were spliced together. I took a pencil and decorated them with mustaches and swastikas. I leafed through the hard news and continued my artwork on other telephotos. I put a nice set of antennae on a foreign minister.

I hadn't properly cooked the egg—the white was runny. I poured on Tabasco sauce and ground dill. I put three spoons of sugar in the coffee. When I had finished I folded up the papers and piled them next to the radiator. A burst of steam caused the metal stopcock to shake and whistle.

I went outside and began walking north toward the

river. The city was flaring up with traffic; ten million people spinning like Catherine wheels, locomoting like pistons and camshafts, racing towards the end of time. I approached London Bridge. In twenty years I'll be old, in fifty I'll be dead, I thought. It didn't make any kind of sense. The sun was warm on my nose, while my cheeks were flushed with cold.

From afar, and in the mind, the bridge appeared old and mythical. Once on it though, you found it had been reinforced and girded through the centuries with common concrete and iron, so it looked like a hundred other bridges, indistinguishable. I stopped in the middle and rested on the railing. I looked eastward to see the Tower of London rising from the ground.

I hoofed it up King William Street to Eastcheap, where I studied a maze of bus routes. A man with a bruised-up camel briefcase stood smoking a pipe at the end of the queue.

"How do I get to the Brompton Cemetery?"

He removed the pipe from his mouth. "A good dose of arsenic often does the trick."

"And by bus?"

"A nine to Earls Court. Change to the thirty-one."

"Thank you."

He rapped the pipe against the signpost to empty it. "Say hello to me mum. Plot 1765-B overlooking the Walham Green. Artificial lilies."

The front door to Parker's building was ajar. Inside, the hallways were stained with light and smelled of lemon. I took the stairs three at a time.

The door to the apartment was painted with angels, burnished gold and red, flying in circles around a Barclays Bank.

Inside, the room was painted black, floor to ceiling. The paint had been lacquered over and over, so that it was glossy and plastic. A number of long spears were stuck in the floor, standing erect; a neon sign, glowing pink and green was hanging on the west wall. It read: INRI.

In the middle of the room Parker was kneeling on the floor applying a coat of varnish to the crossbar of a gigantic wooden crucifix. He wore a ceremonial black hooded cape with black shoes and black gloves. He had shaved off his mustache and wore black lipstick and black sunglasses.

I approached him. He lay down the varnish and began going over a patch of tiny bubbles with a scrap of finely grained sandpaper. The crucifix was encumbered with straps at the three points where nails would be driven to pin a man's body.

"Greetings, fellow suffering son of man," said Parker. He ran the pole of his thumb over the dulled patch of wood. "Come back from the dead to inspire the quick?" He picked up the varnish and dabbed it with a fine brush to the sanded spot. "But tell me, how did you get mixed up with those lords of evil? Playing for keeps—that's hardly true to your form."

"Technical error," I said.

Parker fastened the tin and placed the brush in a jar of thinner. "Technique is the better part of sainthood," he said. "One cannot just whistle and expect the universal forms to fall in line."

"Oh, sure, Parker," I said. "Listen—what are you doing?"

He wet the print of his index finger with his tongue, and held it up in the air. "North by northeast," he muttered. "Eh—what's that? My work ... Our walk through the Brompton Cemetery, your abduction—I saw how our acts in life foreshadow the endings of our lives, that every afternoon we may be practicing up for our deaths." He lowered his finger and looked me over with his graveled face.

"So came the end of white—that universe was closed to me, not just by necessity—more like a convenience, a convenience of fate ... I tumbled back into blackness, that which came first, the alpha, the father and mother of white ... when I returned from Victoria I stayed up the night feverishly altering everything."

He smiled suddenly, showing a line of teeth blackened and gleaming like those rarest pearls.

"Then I began work on my first masterpiece. A large panel, three meters by three—the magic square—depicting the crucifixion of Christ in a supermarket ... The cross rises from the frozen food section, and all the shoppers are on their knees, their heads ringed with crown and nimbus. Christ's blood is dripping from the spot where he has been lanced by Longinus's spear, gathering in a pool on the linoleum ... Grief," he turned his head and held his tongue momentarily between his teeth, "it is awash with modern grief—the loneliness of an old spinster shopping for her paltry supper, the ragman stealing a tin of carrots from the nethermost shelf ..."

I looked across the room. Every thirty seconds the neon sign flashed off and on. My heart felt like a balloon, expanding against my rib cage. I saw the spot on my arm, blue and bruised, where they'd plunged the needle.

Parker left the room, returning with a Hasselblad, a flash device, and a tripod. He set them up on the floor. "Give me a hand with the cross, Eddie."

We lifted the crucifix, then screwed it into a base in front of one of the bays. It stood some nine feet.

Parker dragged a stepladder from the kitchen. He climbed it and pushed his back flush to the cross. "Strap me in."

I stood on my tiptoes and fastened his arms to the crossbars.

He crossed his ankles and I lashed them down with the third thong. "Pull back the stile."

I pulled away the stepladder. I stood at attention and observed Parker on the cross. He said nothing for a long time—his brow was knitted and he tried not to move. Sometimes there was a soft rustle of his cape; his nose would quaver, twittering the sunglasses.

"I am I," he announced. "I am purest black and I am traveling to the all-black. I have taken all precautions—

all the planes of consciousness have been tarred and
sooted, every avenue of experience has been boarded up
and blindfolded. This is the end of modern man—adios,
sayonara, pipe-off—turn to ash and ink, I'm bleeding
black ..."

He seemed short of breath, he huffed on the words. I
watched him squirm.

"How does it feel, Parker?"

"It's hard to breathe. You know, that's what kills you.
You don't bleed to death—you suffocate. The nails are
just for show. I'll take my stigmata between the eyes, if
you don't mind."

He began mumbling to himself. Something about
going "'neath the streets of London," and then some pid-
gin French and a great metaphysical babble and
wordquake in his native idiom.

"Man the cameras, Edward."

I looked through the viewfinder of the Hasselblad.
Parker was clearly focused and centered in the gate. I followed his technical instruction and took a picture; a flash
exploded and lit up the room. I did it seven times.

Later we sat at the kitchen table drinking absinthe and
chasing it with cola. "You're looking out of sorts,
Edward." He poured a dram of absinthe into a black
eggcup and held it between his hands. "Perhaps the
London weather is not agreeing with you."

"I'm having a string of bad luck," I said.

Parker shook his head. He had donned a black
bathrobe and slippers, and seemed incredibly at ease.
"Then you are in deep trouble. For luck is all you ever had.
You best return to Amsterdam; start all over. Hopefully,
the action on the tables didn't go cold in your absence."

"Are you chasing me away?"

He shot down the liquor. He wrinkled up his face, a tear
flowed down from beneath his darkened lenses. "Hale
stuff, this absinthe ... outside of the Iberian Peninsula,
illegal worldwide ... Chasing you away? No, not a bit.
After I develop these photos, true, I shall be occupied

some days on my next work: *St. Mark Preaching in Alexandria*."

"Giovanni Bellini already covered that one," I said. "About four-hundred years ago. It's in Milan."

"Yes, of course," replied Parker. "But instead of preaching to Egyptians, he'll be addressing a group of aliens from Jupiter and Saturn. There will be a center panel, and side panels from the crucifixion, featuring myself as the savior. One of the aliens will be lying on the ground, dreaming about the beheading of John the Baptist."

"I think I have to go," I said.

"Yes. You do."

I walked down Threadneedle Street toward London Bridge, and my body filled with paranoia. I envisioned myself skulking along a fifty-foot wall. Instead of veins, electric strings ran along my arms—there was contact and my bones lit up — a glowing green skeleton.

I'd hit the suckers hard at the Portobello Road that weekend and my wallet held a couple hundred pounds. If my luck was turning now, running kinks in the gyre, it might be time to make a run for it. I'd go home and pack the Gladstone, and take to ground.

I passed Fish Street Hill and began to cross the river. A trepanned boat passed beneath the Tower Bridge. There were two belfries and an orange railing, and the Tower of London, rising like a ghostly chimney.

I looked down Mermaid Court and saw that police cars were lining the curbs. There was a bunch of bulls gathered on the stoops near my flat; the static report of police radios shot down the block.

I turned around and ran as fast as I could. I heard voices shouting and the gunning of engines. I ran through the hospital yards and passed a row of garages with rusted doors. I raced along the Hop Exchange, stone curving, blue and white: Hand Drawn Ales. A train roared overhead on the metal bridge, green signs were hanging from orange girders: it seemed like an ancient circus. A trough in the street held garbage, slow-rotting fruit from the Borough Market.

I ran across Blackfriars Road, hopping over fenders and weaving through traffic. I thought I heard someone behind me calling my name, or one just like it; but I ran all the way to Waterloo Station without looking back.

I rode in the tube back and forth to Paddington, for one hour, then two. I realized that no one was after me, that no one cared about me; I'd played my role and had been sent to the wings to languish in anonymity till the end of days.

On one pass through Baker Street Station a man with skin the color of German umber boarded and sat across the aisle. He had clear liquid eyes that never focused, he wore black second-hand clothes, and his tennis shoes were unlaced. He wore a gold badge over his breast, decorated with a bolt of red lightning. In his hands he held a pile of metal cards, thin as wafers, and went through them one at a time.

When his stop came near he dropped the cards in a pocket. Someone had left some mints of different colors scattered on his seat. He picked a few up, examining them closely, then popped them in his mouth. From the floor, he snatched the wrapper that the candies had come in, crumpled it, and placed it in the pocket with the cards.

It was Parker, I think, or someone else and myself, walking along the Thames. The other man picked up a crescent-shaped stone and glided it sidearm across the water.

"Ever seen God?" he asked.

"No, never," I answered. The stone skipped twice and disappeared, leaving a chain of tremoring webs.

"No, neither me … That's because there is no God, no master plan—nothing … We generated at random from the sea—our grandfathers were trout and salmon: and a bunch of seaweed … The last time I went to the dentist, he removed a third molar and gave me a glass of saltwater to swish about my mouth. I looked at it and cried: 'Pappy dearest!'"

Perhaps it was Lyndon MacBeth, or someone I'd met in a pool hall. We passed back and forth a thick cigarette of West Indian ganja, and toured the rusting hulls of some old pleasure-craft.

"And there're no angels," he pronounced, not with certainty, nor with disrespect. "Just the human mind— become much changed from the trout's, one must admit, a thousand million years of differentiation does wonders for the cerebellum—we can imagine anything, can't we?"

I scratched my head and thought of Raphael's *Marriage of the Virgin at Cana*. Raphael, age twenty-one, painted himself in at the far right of the wedding party. His hat, remarkable, is composed of spheres, and he seems to be holding a crop in his hand.

"And the devil? Yes," went on the man, "he blossoms from man's heart as well. How we dread this knowledge! No God of mercy and forgiveness would slay ten million in the gas chambers and turn them into lampshades. Nor would a God permit others, even Satan himself, to do it."

It grew dark and we climbed up the bank and stood on Hungerford Bridge. A cruise ship floated along the water, lighted soft green and pink. A garland of red and gold bulbs was strung along the far shore, beneath the Royal Festival Hall. We could see Waterloo Bridge, the cupola of a cathedral, and the flux of cars along the embankment. A long balustrade flashed orange.

"It's hard to say," I said.

"Hard to say?"

"Well—sometimes things do seem to be a little bit infinite, don't they?"

He shook his head and pointed at something roiling in the water. There was a mist in the air, a thin fog shrouded all the lights.

"Eternity is time. That's all we know of it. Every second has the potential to be the final one, so every second lasts a hundred thousand years."

He looked at his watch. Three silver arrows revolved on transparent wheels. Perhaps he was wealthy.

"While you blinked your eyes," he said grimly, "the mastodons were here, sir, and passed into extinction." He looked up at me. "You missed it."

We stopped in a café for a cup of coffee. He ordered a pastry with whipped cream, and sliced it into six parts with a knife. We sat at the window and watched the people of the evening glimmer by.

"God is the one who sends us all our money," I said. "He helps our football teams win on Saturday if we're good, and is on the lips of the sole survivors of terrible catastrophes."

"Exactly," he said. He poured a jigger of cognac into our coffees and ate two segments of his pastry. "God is a convenient reference for human wishes. He's an old man with a white beard sitting in a throne chair reading Trollope ..."

Perhaps it was someone I didn't know. He towered above me, I think, and a lizard was tattooed on the inside of his wrist. I hadn't slept for days, and I talked to everyone.

"A human tear," he said, "contains a thousand gods; the word of a child holds the truth of a thousand bibles ... If you love with true love, not romantic love, or the love of a class for itself—but the love of a mother for her child, the love of Mary for Jesus as he expired on the cross ..."

He left me in Coptic Street, or Little Russell. We stood before a window filled with china plates, pink, blue, aqua, deep rose, celadon green. There were lute players, ladies handling bouquets, a porcelain vase with two hands sprouting from its sides. Lights converged, soft smiles, circles within circles, a gypsy in a gilded frame.

He removed a cigarette from his mouth and tossed it to the pavement, splashing sparks. There was a trace of lipstick on his starched shirt.

"All gods are God," he said. "Don't you understand, my liege? The Son of God, the Son of Man ... it's all the same. You are Christ and so am I, and so is every bubble in a piece of ice—it's 'the noise in the street' ..."

"And the evil?"

"We're the evil—and we can destroy it."

"Destroy ourselves."

"No," he said sadly. "You've missed my point." He looked up and turned to go. "But just as well …"

Some time passed. Then, one night, at three a.m., the phone began ringing in my apartment. I woke up out of a dream and couldn't understand what was happening.

The phone continued ringing. I got out of bed and picked it up.

"Yes."

"Hello. Eddie." It was Jana. Her voice was weak and the words came slowly.

"Yes."

"I'm dying, Eddie."

I turned on the light switch. I couldn't remember where I'd put my spectacles. Everything was a mess of pastel.

"Why do you think so?"

"Come and see me."

"You're still in London."

"Please."

"Okay."

She gave me the name of a bed and breakfast on Eccleston Square. I got dressed and tried to brush back my hair. I put in my earrings, and wrapped a wool scarf my mother had given me around my neck. I found my glasses, but not my keys. I left the door unlocked.

The moon was out and dogs were running in the street. I saw a shadow flicker in the gutter: a rat, or an hallucination. It was bitterly cold and there was a slicing wind. I didn't have any gloves and my knuckles burned.

I found a night bus in Eastcheap and rode to Trafalgar Square. The sad dregs of the nighttime were gathered, silent, waiting for their buses. Everything was hard and bleak, the moonshine over lamplight, the calls and alarums of the drunk and the stunned.

The hotel smelled faintly of cat piss. The deskman, thin as a walking stick, baffled and watching television, tried to say something to me. I walked past him and took the stairs two at a time.

The walls and the woodwork were clean; the carpet was thick and lusterless, stained and bleached the color of pale tea. On the fourth landing, a nude man with long hair walked out of the communal shower.

Jana's room was on the sixth landing. I stood at the door and tried to gain back my breath. Down the hall a song called 'Wuthering Heights' was playing on the radio.

I turned the knob and walked in. The room was small, a garret, with the far wall sloped. There was a narrow bed, a dark-wood armoire, a sink and a chair. A single window, the size of a shoebox, was set in next to the ceiling.

Jana was lying on top of the bed, propped up on pillows. She was wearing a madras bathrobe and white cotton socks. Her face, pale and wiped of make-up, had several welts on it. The bone beneath her right eye was bruised—violet and swollen. An unlit cigarette hung between her fingers.

I sat down next to her on the spread. Her eyes were red, the lids puffed-up, her gaze without expression. She seemed to be looking at a spot across the universe.

"Can you light my cigarette, please? The matches are by the sink."

The basin was scratched and dulled with scouring. Beneath it there was a tiny gray wastebasket brimming with balled-up tissue. I found the matches next to a white biscuit of soap.

Jana's hand trembled while she pushed the cigarette to her lips. She cupped the back of my wrist to anchor the match against the tobacco. She let go of me, closed her eyes and filled her lungs with smoke. She held it in, luxuriating in it for many seconds before dispelling it in the air.

I sat back down next to her and brushed her hair away from her neck. There was a v-shaped contusion on her throat. She touched me again, her hand faltering. Several of her nails were broken, and the polish was cracked.

A distant whirr of traffic ebbed in through the slice of window. A door slammed down the hall, and we heard some people screaming in Arabic. Jana took another lug on the cigarette. The smoke came out a faded pink.

"Under the bed there is a bag, Eddie. Take it up."

I reached beneath the bed and pulled out a small plaid suitcase. It was made of heavy cloth and festooned with zippers. A yellow tag was attached to the handle. It bore a name I didn't know and an address on the Eppendorfer Weg in Hamburg.

"Open it."

I pulled back the central zippers and lifted the top half. The bag was filled with fifty-pound notes, bundled together with red twine. I looked beneath the top sheaves, riffling through with my fingers to the bottom. It was all the same—

"That's a lot of looey," I said.

A faint smile passed Jana's face, and then it turned cold as flint and steel again. Her eyes covered with rheum, the pupils expanded until they engulfed the diaphragms of the irises. Another door slammed and there was more shouting.

"Why don't you take it," whispered Jana, "and run far away." She blinked her eyes and turned her face.

I took the cigarette from her and tipped the ashes onto the rug. I took a puff, just so that I could taste her lips, then returned it to her fingers.

"It seems too easy," I said.

Jana rested the cigarette on the edge of the night-stand. She edged herself a little farther up on the pillows and pulled up the madras bathrobe tight to her throat. In the bad lamplight her face was pocked with shadows, and her platinum hair was streaked with black.

"Are you frightened of the easy, Eddie?" she said.

I looked at the pile of money. The colors were pretty, and the designs were palatable, not intended to displease.

I thought of a burning house, bright yellow and purple flames; a bag of diamonds dropping down into a cool lake.

"Whose money is this?" I asked.

"What do you mean?"

"Where does it come from?"

Jana pinched the glowing end of the cigarette between her fingers. She held it without flinching until the fire died. "It comes from blood," she said. She released the butt end and touched her fingertips to her tongue. "It comes from blood and goes to blood. That is the name of money. It belongs to everybody. Don't you see?"

"No ... not really."

She rubbed her fingertips across her forehead, crossing the furrow with wet ash. She threw her head back and folded her palms in her lap.

"The money is blood," she said in a monotone, "and we bleed all the same—dark blue inside, like the nighttime sky, pouring out into the air, bright red like rubies. Often we can change it from one body to the next, one pocket to the next, from the gutter to the bank, from the murderer to the king."

She blinked her eyes to keep away the tears. There was glitter on her lashes, and in the murky light it seemed like tiny twinkling stars. Her life was bigger than mine; my being was dwarfed, diminished by her chaos.

"Did you sell Werner's weight to Lyndon MacBeth?"

She looked away from me and made a crude, derisive sound. "I don't know what you're talking of, man!" She spat the words out, staccato, and looked back at me, glaring, red in the face. "I ask you again. Are you afraid of this money? What is it? A million pounds? It's nothing, nothing, I'm telling you ... It's worth one bomb that your government dropped on Vietnam, a tiny splash of shit and death.

"And Werner? Werner is nobody, nobody at all. He is making always his own death dreams, we do not have to help him in this ..."

"But still—"

"But still!" she snapped, suddenly sitting up. "But still you are looking into something very small—only to make it something very big, to make it important—but it is nothing, nothing … Throw this fucking bag out of the window. Do you think it matters now? Take it to the church and feed it to Jesus Christ and his priests … It isn't life, Eddie. It's blood outside the body, red, not blue … It's nothing … nothing."

Exhausted by her tirade, she leaned back on the pillows. I pushed my hair back with one hand, then the other, applying a great deal of pressure. I pulled my glasses up on top of my head for a moment. The light of the lamp was nearly unbearable; Jana's face was as white as chalk.

"What should I do with it?" I asked.

"Take it back to Holland," she answered in a weak voice.

I stood up and walked across the little room. A narrow full-length mirror hung next to the armoire. The frame was broken in several places, and the silvering was peeling off behind the glass. I saw myself, and Jana behind me; her head seemed disembodied, rising above my shoulder. I thought that maybe I was living out my life in a mirror, that fate was only what was reflected next to me at the moment.

"Then what?"

She closed her eyes and mouth and respired several times through the nose. Her chest pulsed, and her arms jerked faintly at the elbows. "In the pocket of the bag," she said weakly. "There is a key with a number scratched on it … It is for a luggage box in the Centraal Station in Amsterdam … Lock this bag in the box."

Her eyes opened and there was a look of vague terror in them. "You must do that for me, Eddie. You are the last one … Can you?" She began crying in earnest, tears swimming down her cheekbones onto the bedding. "Please."

"Okay," I said.

Feebly, she patted at the mattress. "Come, lie with me a moment."

I went over and stretched out next to her on the bed. She pushed her wet face to mine, and touched her lips to my neck. I felt her breasts pressed against my chest. My throat contorted and everything was moving far away.

"Will I see you again?"

"Don't ask such a thing like this, Eddie," she said hoarsely, talking in my ear. "Yes, in a few days I will find you again, after I gather back my strength." She put her foot on my ankle, and with her finger, she traced a secret sign on my palm.

"The key?"

"Get rid of it. There is a washroom next to the luggage boxes. Flush it away. I have another ..." She squeezed my hand. "Do you love me, Eddie?"

She became still. Her breathing was labored and irregular. Everything else was quiet; the street, the halls. I couldn't imagine ever leaving.

"Do you love me Eddie?"

"No one can love you," I said.

"Even if we are in the bubble together ... even if I come to you always when you think it is finished, even if your name is on my lips when I have the black dreams?'

"I don't know," I said. I put my arms around her and thought of things from long before. Outside a clock chimed the quarter hour; something dark, a bat or a small bird, bumped at the window and was repelled.

"My heart is in a box," she whispered. "It is locked always from the inside—no one can break in ... I am riding with you on the carpet, this it says in the middle dreams, before the black ones come ... The morning lights are coming soon—then you must go, but I keep you in mind, and me in yours, in the bubble floating up ... no one can take it ..."

She began talking quickly, then in spurts and stops, in a language I didn't understand. I let myself go with her into the outskirts of her world, holding tightly to the barrier between the two gates. Our breathing was together, and purple sparks passed between my eyes. I saw many shades of white and long filaments of silver. We lay in each other's arms for some time.

I fixed my clothes and buttoned my coat.

"Climb up the stairs and you will find the roof," said Jana. She turned on her side so that I could not see her face. "It fastens to the next building, another place like this. Better to leave from there. Go now. The black time is beginning again."

PART III

One week later, I was walking toward the Leidsestraat at three in the afternoon. It was unseasonably warm, and the narrow street was jammed with people. A trolley rolled down the middle of the pavement, screamed around the corner and over the next canal.

I walked up the bridge and stared down the line of the waterway. A café owner was setting up round white tables outside the shop. A young girl with long blonde hair followed him out with a brace of slatted chairs, a tablecloth folded over her arm.

I walked on and turned down a pedestrian lane cramped on either side with low buildings. Many of the shutters on the second floor were open, and from one I heard the sound of a cello followed by a chorus of voices.

I pulled back a brass ring on a slab of scarred oak and negotiated the doorway of the Bar Europa. An old bulletin board of cork was plastered with colored flyers, advertisements of concerts, strange meetings, word of lost dogs and cheap apartments to seek or let.

I climbed the rotting stairs, a thrill in my heart, and the smell of beer and hashish pierced my nose. The light grew dimmer, and the sound of an old jukebox carried down from above.

There were few people in the main hall. Two morose men sat at the bar looking into tarnished tankards. The bartender was engaged in taking down each bottle of liquor from the mirrored shelving, and wiping it clean of dust. Most of the long rows of tables were abandoned. A nervous looking man in sunglasses and ill-fitting coat, stood over the jukebox, studying the glass top.

I sat down at a table in a corner, beneath a picture of a zeppelin, and put my boots up on a chair. From the loudspeaker, a coda of static followed the end of one song, and then another tune came over, an old number that recalled my adolescence, when the words of a song were the words of God.

A boy with his hair tied back in a ponytail approached me. He rested his hands on the table, and smiled dully. He wore a dangling heart-shaped earring in the left lobe and his denim jacket was pierced with hundreds of six-pointed metal studs. He hesitated to speak, as if waiting for his brain to catch up with his body.

"Do you like something to smoke?" he said at last, in a thick Latin accent.

"What do you have?'

He pulled out a long thin leather purse, fine-tooled with geometric designs and feathered along the edges, from beneath his jacket, and lifted the apron. There were many sleeved compartments inside, each filled with small plastic packages.

"I have everything," he said. He probed the purse with long tapered fingers, checking the arrangements of the packets, pushing one up suddenly with his thumb, then letting it fall in.

"I have blond Lebanese with the PLO stamp, green African from Angola, marvelous buds from the liberated Ho Chi Minh City. We have CIA inspected shit from the Laos Hmong, Thai sticks of course, Moroccan kif from the King's private distillation, a taste of red Hawaiian if you don't like ever to come back."

He gave me a cool glance and kissed the tips of his thumb and forefinger.

"Anything black?"

"Yes, why not. Black Kashmiri. It is dangerous."

He lifted out a packet from an inner sleeve and flipped it to me. I split the vacuum seal and pushed it to my nose. "No thanks," I said. I dropped it back in his purse.

His face grew solemn. He picked the discarded product from the bag and obsessively wrapped it back up. He shook his head and clucked his tongue.

"You have to be cool, man," he offered. "The nose is not the only guide. Here see this. Now you have the answer." He took out another package enclosing a thin sheet of reddish gold. He spread the lips of the plastic and tendered it to my nose.

"Yes, my friend," he said soothingly. "Here we pick the seeds ourselves from our own South American species, and growing them in our localized gardens near Delft. The cannabis is taken then to Tunis for processing, and shipped back by first air express."

"All right." I took out my billfold and removed twenty-five guilders.

"It is double price." He rapped on the table with his knuckles and returned his purse beneath his jacket. "Make sure you are sitting in a chair when you bang it."

I gave him the fifty guilders and he wandered off into the next room. I shook the lamina of hashish from the bag and placed it between my fingers. I held it beneath my nose once more, then bit off a third. I ground it into my teeth, relishing the acrid taste.

I hailed a barmaid and ordered a pint of the dark beer. While I waited for her I looked at the three-pointed chandeliers and remembered the Trinity paintings I'd seen in the cathedrals in Lima. All the images were painted in triplicate, three faces, three haloes, three doves shooting light at the forehead.

I had been drinking for about half an hour, when I began to feel the effects of the hashish. It was far stronger than I had anticipated. I began melting down into the chair; the force of gravity trying to suck me through the floor. The interior of my skull expanded, and it was hard to remember if I cared about anything, if the last was the first, if the heathens would still rage ...

I left a five guilder note on the table, stood up and wobbled towards the exit. The blood ran down from my head; I felt a long wave of vertigo, colored spots danced exotically across my field of vision.

I descended the stairs. I felt a great love in my heart — a

false love, but still a great one—and I felt for a moment that I was the true center of the universe, the inheritor of the godhead, King Shit Almighty himself.

Outside, the day had nearly disappeared. The sky was darkening overhead, and the small buildings that flanked me were changing in hue. I leaned against the wall and watched the sons of mankind coming and going down the pedestrian walk. My body was overpowered with urges that wouldn't be defined.

I crossed the bare expanse of the Dam plaza as the last fingers of sunlight loosened from the spires of the great cathedral. Fifty people sat in the square in groups of three and five. Some had sleeping bags spread over the concrete, others drank from flasks of cheap wine or played tinny songs on scotched-up guitars. Farther on a man began to juggle sticks of fire. He had a long grizzled beard and wore a silver tunic, and in the twilight he appeared to be a prophet of the late winter night.

I walked down the Damrak past a department store fronted with ancient brick. I advanced to the door; a man in a yellow sweater and thin tie stepped out of a shadow behind the glass and locked up with a jangling ring of keys.

I stopped at a tourist kiosk and looked at postcards on a spinning metal rack. I squinted beneath my sunglasses, trying to make out the forms of the buildings across the canal. The evening traffic splashed down the sidewalk, the worn returning home in the dusk, happy to be free again.

I crossed the bridge over the waters of the Damrak as the light drained from the sky. The street lamps were on, twinkling in the faces of those who passed me by. I looked back over the water, at the great bustle of the city, the buildings of the Middle Ages, the wide sidewalks where Spinoza and Hobbema crossed the paths of the Iconoclasts and Anabaptists; at men in evening dress darting by on bicycles, at princes of Afghanistan and Sierra Leone speeding off in taxis to the airport to catch an evening flight to Peshawar or Ougadougou.

I passed into darker, older streets. A cobbled half-moon lane ran behind a stout medieval church. I looked up at the band of minarets surrounding the steeple, the pigeons huddled on cornices above the Gothic windows. A gold clock was emblazoned on the faraway belfry. Around the curve of the low brick buildings short red bars of neon hung in pairs, with signs for bedrooms to rent.

I walked out onto the Voorburgwal and threaded my way through the side streets that bridged the canals. The air was cut with the smell of sweet, greasy foods; marquees burned with neon, handwritten signs promised strange pleasures. Two drunken soldiers climbed onto a motor scooter and rode away, hugging a path just a foot from the water.

In a murky alley I stopped in front of a glass show window. A prostitute, her back to me, was sitting on a white couch talking on the telephone. The soft pink lights spread a dull glaze on her parlor.

Someone tapped me softly on the shoulder. "Hello," said a theatrical female voice. "Are you looking for a date?"

I put my hands in my pockets and turned around. The woman was back lit in the neon, so that her face was shadowy and blurred. Her features that I could perceive were caked in make-up, her lips painted deep bluish-red, her eyes ringed with shadow, her cheeks rouged. She wore heavy strands of pearls around her neck; a satin blouse was low-cut, her breasts cantilevered out, underpinned with a bone bodice. Her skirt was cut high above the knee, the shoes were of snakeskin with high, razor heels—her legs were silken and long and fashioned by the devil.

She turned her face into the stream of a pale lamp. Her eyes were hard and glazed beneath a gelid smile. She was dressed all different, out of key, and something had happened ... but it was the blonde wig that had caused me not to recognize her at once, under the paint and masquerade.

"Margo," I said quietly. I took her hand: it was cool and barely with reflex. I looked at her again, she was thinner by ten pounds, and the human fire was nearly doused. Her perfume was no longer scented of flowers: it was cloying and laced with malady.

"Oh," she said, her voice softening by a trace, "it is you." Without expression, she brushed her finger across my lips. "I thought you had left us."

A group of oriental men stopped in front of the window. One of them knocked abruptly on the glass. The prostitute hung up the phone and straightened her short dress. She walked across the room and opened the door.

I kept my grip on Margo's hand. We stared at each other as if we were looking into a mirror.

"Where's Jana?" I asked her.

"Jana is gone," she said coldly.

The men began a heated discussion with the prostitute. She began shooting them hard numbers, imitating their strident English.

"What do you mean?"

"Back to Switzerland—with the gypsies." She shrugged her shoulders and crisped her lip. "I don't know." She hesitated. "That's all over now. That's a long time. I have to go."

She tried to pull away her hand. The woman behind the glass waved her finger at the entourage. They laughed and made her a counteroffer. She shook her head haughtily, they spotted her a few points. She acquiesced. The lot of them walked properly in, removing their hats. She pulled shut the curtain and the scene disappeared, leaving only dull pink light.

"Don't you have one moment?"

"I have many moments," said Margo. "But they are not for gifts—they are for sale."

"How much is an hour?"

She looked down at the street. Momentarily, the veneer slipped from her face, she looked faintly concerned, pensive. "An hour is a long time. It would be six hundred guilders."

A group of French tourists, male and female passed us. They were pressed closely together, and laughing nervously. They were speaking about their dinner, a casserole, a side of bacon, a bunch of grapes in a tureen.

"How about four hundred. That's all I have. For a friend."

She shook her head. A garish sequined bag hung from a colored string around her wrist. She twirled it in a tight arc and caught it in her hand.

"There are no more friends," she said. "I do not belong to me anymore."

"A man owns you?"

"No—not that." She looked at me uncomfortably, and wrung her hands. "Something else owns me, it's not a man or a woman or a beast. It's not even an idea. It's dark and frightening, but we have no longer any name for it, in the modern time—in the age of man ..."

She took me by the arm and led me down the street, past a Turkish grocer, and a gangrenous club with a green bulb above the red one. We went into a side-street, darker still. The pavement was dirt; a wild, hungry dog ran past us, kicking up dust, barking rapidly, without purpose. We passed beneath a lamppost that was scrawled with graffiti.

We took a corner, and the street lit up. We walked past a restaurant that smelled of couscous and lamb, into a narrow interstice that cleft two buildings, and stopped before a door.

Margo unclasped her purse and fished out a ring of keys anchored to a whistle. "What happened to your store?" I asked.

"The government shut it."

"Taxes?"

"Taxes," she said mockingly. "Oh yes sure."

It was very dark and Margo fumbled some time with the lock, turning it several times the wrong way before reversing the direction.

"Eddie, you're on the level?" She paused, holding the knob in her hand. "You have money to pay me; it's no bull-shit?"

"It's straight."

She pressed open the door and pushed a glowing button to engage the lights. We were in a closed hallway, at the bottom of a sheer staircase.

"Give it to me."

I counted out four hundred guilders.

"One more."

"That's all I have."

I followed her up the staircase. The runner was new and the walls freshly painted. English hunting scenes hung on the walls in dark narrow frames. We stopped at the third landing. In the brighter light, Margo's face was a hundred times worse.

"Okay, Eddie," she said. "I mean it, no bullshit, nothing. We go in, we talk, we fuck, we pray, one hour—that's it, finished, out..."

We went down the hall to the second room. The door was painted forest green, a polished brass knocker was screwed into the wood. Margo opened the lock with her keys and stepped through the doorway. The light in the hallway was on a timer, and suddenly it turned off. There was no light inside the room either; Margo guided me in by the elbow and shut the door behind us.

"Are you frightened, Eddie?" she whispered.

"I don't know."

"Well, you should be then," said a man's voice.

The lights turned on. Werner Brandt sat on a long velvet sofa, his feet up on a low white table. He was dressed in a serge suit with a red bow tie, his hair was cropped short; he sported a mustache, thin and waxed. A long bone-handled switchblade, inlaid with onyx and studded with colored jewels, was balanced in his palm.

"Welcome to the nightmare," he said. He depressed the button of the knife, and the blade swung out with a hiss. I turned quickly to lunge for the door.

"Stop him, you stupid bitch!" screamed Werner. He jumped to his feet and leapt over the coffee table. As I grabbed the door handle Margo kicked me in the balls with the pointed toe of her shoe. I saw a lambent purple smudge and a whipcord skewered my belly. I fell to the ground wincing and holding my groin.

"*Ja*. Now we take care of you."

He stood over me, skimming the blade of the knife along the fat of his palm. "*Ja*. Now we go right inside you." He reared back his right leg and kicked me in the ribs.

Margo grabbed him by the shoulder. "I'm sorry, Eddie. I'm sorry. Please ... Werner ... not like this ..."

Werner's eyes burned with indignity. "Let me go, bitch. Do you hear!"

Margo released her grip and took a step back. She was about to say something else when Werner cocked his left arm and punched her. "Stay away from this you stupid cunt!" She crumpled to the floor clutching at her belly.

Werner grabbed me by the wrist and pulled my arm behind my back, hoisting my fingers up to the shoulder blade. He did it slowly, pulling back half an inch at a time until I screamed. His knee dropped onto my back, pinning me to the floor, and with the other hand he held the blade of the knife to my neck. He put his mouth close to my ear, so that I could feel his breathing.

He waited a few moments. I couldn't turn my head, but I could hear Margo sobbing, taking short breaths. "You know, Eddie," said Werner, in a gentle mannered voice, "they say that money makes the world go round. Do you know that?" His breath was warm against my ear, and smelled of garlic and gin. "Well?"

"Yes." Bolts of pain shot up my shoulder. I clamped my teeth tightly to keep from screaming again.

"So," he said gently, "tell me where the money is."

He pulled my arm higher arching me backwards. He raised his knee, and then slammed me forward smashing my face into the floorboard. I turned my head just enough to avoid breaking my nose. Blood came seeping from my mouth, flowing up towards my eye.

"It's still ... in London."

"It's still in London!" He pulled up on my arm again; the bone felt like it was going to snap. He dug his knee into my spine again.

"It's still in London!" he shouted in my ear. "You bloody fucking ass. We might as well call in the priest for you now," he whispered. "Yes, back to the square one ... A nice cold home under the ground ..."

I breathed slowly through my teeth, looking out across the floor through my twisted glasses. I stared at the grain of the wood; the blood seeped along it in little furrows. Margo's crying was dimmer, and muffled. Once or twice I heard her shudder.

Werner put the knife to my throat again. "Where is it?'

"In my room."

"In the hotel?"

"Yes."

He removed the knife from my throat and raised his knee from my back. It made me feel like I was flying. "Don't move," he said. "Not an inch. I have to think."

His shoes had taps on the toes and I could follow the sound of his pacing across the floor. "Get up, Margo." He said something vulgar in German. "Get up off your ass. Make some coffee and some brandy. There's water on the stove, already hot. We must make a new plan."

Margo rose soundlessly; I could barely hear her crossing the room. As she entered the kitchen, she passed before my field of vision . Her eyes were red, the make-up smeared across her face. Her head was drooped, her arms hung lifelessly at her sides.

When she disappeared Werner kicked me wildly in the kidney. I caught my breath; my body jerked like an eel. I tried to grip the floor with my hands to push myself up. He kicked me again in the ribs and I collapsed.

"Sorry we have missed you in Schiphol," he said, standing tall above me. His words vibrated oddly, as if they were enveloped in gas. "The airport security was strong that day, we could not give you a welcome home party. You have escaped us so far by luck ... Where is the loot, boy? Where is it?"

He grabbed me by the hair and pulled my head back, my chin lifted several inches off the ground. My glasses fell to the floor, and everything was blurred. He pulled further back, at a sharp angle; my neck was ready to break.

"Do you like it better this way? Or with the knife to the throat? Maybe both is best?" I felt the cold metal against my larynx. Everything seemed like it would end in a moment.

"Why are you here *still*, Eddie? I am shaking my head, because I think I must be dreaming. No, I say to myself, he couldn't still be here. I will open my eyes and he will be gone... But no, here you are ... still .... But wait ... one more thing to think about ..."

He slid the knife off my throat and relaxed his grip on my hair. There were all manner of blue and purple spots blinking in front of me. Then I felt the blade forced between my legs, the tip of it pressed to my crotch.

"Now what do you say, skipper? Do you remember where the money is. You fucking scum. Where is the money?" He pressed the knife deeper. "I'll feed your testicles to the goldfish. Can you understand?" He began to scream. "Now tell me! Tell me!" Then in a livid rage, "Now tell me! You—"

I felt something stinging on the back of my neck. Werner gave a blood-curdling shriek, a cry of intense agony—all the pain of life. He let go of my hair and continued to scream. The knife thudded to the floor.

I was in shock. Pushing with my palms, I slowly turned myself in an arc, revolving on my knees like a wounded dog.

Werner was lying on his back, holding his hands to his eyes. His ears and forehead, his hair and shirt, were all wet and bright red. Margo stood stiffly at his side, one hand perched on her hip, the other holding the handle of a black flatiron, the soleplate smeared with blood. Wisps of steam rose from the ports.

Werner writhed on the floor, groaning. Slowly, Margo lowered herself to her knees. Her face was frozen, catatonic, the mad garish make-up tinting her like a harlequin. She clutched the flatiron as if it weighed but an ounce, and began flogging Werner mercilessly with it about the skull, over and over.

He tried to fight it off at first—he looked pathetic, his eyes bone-white and blinded, his hands held weakly above his head as the blows rained down and his crown covered with thick red liquid.

"Die! die—he won't die!" screamed Margo. There was blood all over her blouse and hands; it was smeared across her cleavage and spattered on her shoes. Her face contorted with rage.

"I can't kill him, no! I can't kill him! This head will grow back with nine more ... Go away, go away, go back to your cage in hell, never come back!"

Werner slumped to the floor, his cheek lying in a pool of blood. Margo continued flailing him—more weakly though, the flatiron growing heavy; hitting at his shoulder, at his back and arms, over and over, like a creaking machine that wouldn't turn off, as if she could never stop the cycle.

Finally she dropped the instrument. She lay on the ground next to him, out of breath.

I crawled along the floor and rested my back against the edge of a tall chiffonnier. I untwisted my spectacles and fitted them to the wings of my nose; I grimaced and massaged my shoulder with my fingertips. Shooting pains ran up my neck, my back felt like it was nailed with spikes, the glands of my throat were engorged with lymph.

Margo remained motionless on her back. Her eyes were open, her hands folded over her sternum, her legs strangely tangled.

"How are you?" I asked.

"I need some dope," she said mechanically.

"Is that all?"

"No," she said. "That's not all. A million things more." She rocked slowly from side to side and straightened her legs. Her hair was unfurled and lay out flat on the floor.

"But that's the best I can hope to get," she continued in a monotone. "It's the only dream that I can make come true ... I'm too frightened to find the others ... do you comprehend—it's not in my hands: I let go of my destiny a long time ago. The weavers of fate have sewn my brain shut ..."

Slowly, I got to my feet. I limped over to where Werner lay. He was a gruesome sight, his left temple caved in, his hair and collar enveloped in blood. I knelt down and held up his wrist. There seemed to be a faint reading; my own nerve endings were throbbing too much to really tell.

"Please, Eddie, no!" said Margo. She propped herself up at the elbows. Her face radiated horror. "Leave him dead, leave him dead."

Suddenly his eyes popped open. Margo screamed. She collapsed again and buried her face with her hands. "Oh my God no!"

I watched his lips twitching, he was trying to say something. I put my ear close to his mouth.

"What is it, Werner?"

His lips stopped grinding. His eyeballs began moving furiously in the sockets, darting back and forth like a fish. A deep groan came from his chest and a glob of blood spurted out from his mouth.

His eyes moved once more, then again, telegraphing their final message before they froze in place. I dropped his wrist, and made the sign of the cross.

I pulled Margo up to a sitting position. I put my arms around her and held her crudely blazoned face to my own. She began weeping, holding her body rigid, her elbows tight at her sides. The tears glided over my skin, and when I closed my eyes they felt like blood.

"He's dead," I said.

She started shaking. She unknotted her fingers and dug the nails into my forearms. "Where did he go?"

"I don't know," I said.

"Somebody must know." Her body was convulsing, she dug her nails in deeper.

"Who?" I said.

I sat on the davenport while Margo took a shower. I tried to pick my way through an article in *Il Messagero* about a scandal in the Milan stock market. I lost the thread of reasoning, if there was any, and set the paper down on the cushion.

The sitting room of the apartment was formal and forbidding. The thick suede that covered the armchairs was unsullied by human touch, the exotic furniture woods were unmarred, retaining all the luster of the factory. The mahogany floor was dotted with Persian throw rugs; the walls were the deep green of the nineteenth century, trimmed at the ceiling with cherry-dark moldings.

Werner's corpse lay on the floor, draped with a silk sheet. The fabric billowed up surreally at his face and toes.

Margo entered the room. She was dressed in a black messaline suit with cuffs flued and rose piping at the neck. She wore a white fur cape and a triangular hat. She kept her eyes averted from the cadaver, as she drew on a pair of long thin gloves. Her face was excessively made up, as before, and as waxen as a candle. A newspaper bundle was tucked beneath her arm.

"Could you please take care of this?" She held out the package.

I got up from the couch and approached her. "What is it?'

"My shoes ... I cannot remove the stains."

"The rest?"

"I can take care of the rest."

"Everything?" I said, receiving the bundle.

"Hurry up and get out."

She went to the door, undid the chain and held it open for me. There was a full-length mirror aside the jamb, and as I left I caught her reflection, the ghastly face atop the perfect body, as if it had been attached as a replacement for the original.

There was a chute for trash at the bottom of the staircase. I pulled it open but I couldn't bear to part with my gift. I looked down into the bottomless mouth, then let go the handle.

Outside, the dawn was approaching. I walked quickly down the sidewalk into the dim light. I caught a whiff of smoked meat, and there was a scarlet thread, and then it began to snow, slowly at first, fat wet flakes, and then, of a sudden, the skies were caked with white, and I could only see a few feet in front of me as I took the bridge over a canal.

In my hotel room I sat at the desk and unraveled the newspaper package. I removed the shoes carefully from their bunting, setting them up on their heels on the blotter. Midnight blue bows were fastened to the vamps of the toes, and the straps were painted with zebra stripes. I picked one up and held it in my hand like a tiny animal.

It did not seem fair that things had escaped my control like this; that scattered events, fleeting and spare instants of emotion, would skewer my life, and turn it in such unforeseen ways. I had meant for things to remain random forever.

I'd led my life in bluster and bluff, one step forward and two to the side, escaping always in the inky haze of the cuttlefish. It always seemed to work for me, and always I could keep moving, skipping in space from stone to stone, while the world trembled and the earth collapsed.

But now I was in that dream, trying to run, and my legs were fastened down in a strange bog, and I could barely raise them. I was hollow inside, a far-ranging vacuum, and I saw my sister lying in her coffin, a rose-orange tint on her cheeks, and I guess, well, I guess I don't know ...

I stood up and looked through the narrow window.

There was a blizzard over Amsterdam, the snow beat against the glass with a thousand and one little fists. I grabbed the sash with my fingers and forced open the pane. Outside it was howling white, I couldn't see to the other side of the courtyard. Icy splinters splashed my face.

Behind me, in the hall, there came a sound of shouting, then angry beating on the door. I stood still, motionless, there was nowhere to go.

A key turned in the lock, and the door pushed open. There was rasping of iron and wood: the chain caught in the hasp.

"Quickly! Open up. It is the police!"

I threw the shoes out the window; I heard them ricocheting on the brick as I closed the pane. Someone began kicking at the door.

I wiped my face on the bedspread. "I'm coming."

I unfastened the chain. Inspector van Velden pushed his way past me into the room followed by the heavy-set, oafish constable. "Put the handcuffs on him."

The constable pulled the chair out from beneath the desk and grunted something in Dutch. He pushed me to the seat and wrapped my arms around the back of it. He unfastened a pair of plated handcuffs from his gunbelt and clamped them on my wrists, threading the link through the spindles of the chair.

Van Velden sat down opposite me on the bed. He was dressed in a double-breasted aubergine suit, a twill waistcoat, a thin stippled necktie. He removed his hat and set it on his lap, and crossed his legs precisely on the knee. His movements were lithe and fey.

"You can leave the room, Groot ... Whew it's cold in here. Why have you opened the window, Verlaine? Are you filled with drugs again?"

The lackey left the room. Van Velden flipped his hat in the air—it spun and landed flat on the desk, startling me. He looked at me quizzically.

"So you are back in our town, Verlaine. You are very

stupid then—you did not listen to me. You were best to stay in London— it is a big city, too big for a little shit like you to be noticed ..."

I tested the tension of the handcuffs. The bull had fastened them very tight, and my wrists were burning. The window was still open a crack and a sheet of cold air spread across the room. I shivered.

"Why are you following me?"

Van Velden took a green box from his waistcoat and nicked open the lid with his thumbnail. "There is no need to follow you," he said. "You leave a trail of your shit wherever you go ... Smoke?" He tapped the packet against his palm; a purple cheroot jumped up.

"No."

He leaned back until his head rested on the pillow. He pulled up his feet and settled his shoes on the spread so that the soles were pointing at my face.

"You're in a great bit of trouble." He raised a jet of fire from a thin lighter. Flecks of gold were imbedded in the irises of his eyes; the whites were clear, and as opaque as milk.

He lit the cheroot.

"I said you're in trouble."

"I heard you ... Maybe if you spoke faster."

He took a drag and exhaled a lazy line of smoke, curling it off the lower lip. "You have become impatient since last we met."

"There's nothing left to wait for."

I heard a faraway ringing in my ears and my face felt flushed, the blood rising to the surface of the skin. I felt some bizarre love for van Velden, and then I wished to destroy him.

"What do you want?"

"The money," he said. "That's all."

"The money?"

"Yes ... The money. The green stuff. You remember that?"

No one spoke and the seconds passed very slowly. The

room thickened with smoke. Van Velden was frozen in repose, a hand resting on the knee, his eyes unblinking, a long unbroken wisp flagging his cigarette.

"Why do you want it?"

"It is evidence."

"Of what?"

"Why," he said—he tapped a knurl of ash onto my sheet —"it is evidence of motion."

"The what ..."

"It shows the motion of crime."

He sat up on the edge of the bed. He looked at me sharply.

"All crime leads to money, you see ... Prostitution, arson, murder, mayhem, theft ... drugs—everything. So what do we *do* about that?"

He hoisted two fingers, cutting the air as with scissors, pointing them at me. "We start with the money, is what we do ... and follow its journey backwards ... the twists and the turns, the ugly dancing ... backwards, backwards ... until we arrive at last at the crime. You understand, Eddie. It's very simple."

Van Velden slid his hand within his jacket and came out holding a .38 Webley. He stood up and took a step towards me, pointing the gun at the bridge of my nose.

"Where's the money?"

"In the mattress. It's sewn up. You'll have to cut it open."

Van Velden paused for a moment, thinking, keeping the heater leveled at my face. "Life or death," he said. "What shall it be? I can't decide."

He reached behind the chair and unlocked the handcuffs. He took a step back. I looked up and stared at him, rubbing my wrists. His hand hovered over the lapel of his jacket.

"Groot!"

The constable stepped heavily into the room. His mouth was partly open, and his cheeks hung lobed with fat.

"Take him to the car and wait for me," ordered van Velden. "I want to search the room."

"Yes."

"Have someone look in the yard there. See what he dropped from the window.... Come on, Verlaine. Get."

I stood up and the bull grabbed me by the upper arm. I tried to resist him, he shoved me at the shoulder.

"Where are you taking me?"

"We're going to put you in jail," said van Velden.

"Why?"

"You're a suspect."

I felt my stomach turning. The constable marched me crudely across the room.

"Of what?"

"The murder of Werner Brandt."

I lay on the mattress and looked at the wall. There were crudely lettered phrases scratched on it in all the languages of Babel. There was a cartoon: a swastika dangling from a hangman's noose. A hole at the edge of the ceiling let in a few gasps of fresh air; a weak light bulb hung overhead.

I tried not to think about what was happening. Jail time is dead time. When I felt myself becoming despondent, I trundled onto the floor and did pushups and yogic cobras until I was ready to collapse.

Every few hours there was a sound of clicking boots. A metal grating on the bottom of the door swung open and a tray was pushed in. Usually it was a bowl of thin oatmeal with a piece of cheese floating upon it, and a tin cup with coffee. I ate the food slowly so I wouldn't get nauseated.

There was a Dutch bible in the room, balanced on the pipes beneath the sink. I turned to the Book of Luke and tried to guess at the meaning of the sentences. For some reason, when they emptied my pockets, they left me with my pen, and I underlined some of the text.

I skipped to the walk at Golgotha and began reading aloud. They couldn't take the words from you, the fucks.

They could stick your head in a sack of shit and raise the pliers to your nuts, but the words remained your exclusive possession. They could push your life through a sieve so that you came out in little flakes; they could walk you to the gallows over and over, in dreams and in waking. But the words lived on past your life, an arrow shot through the far length of time, striking a distant object in the future, drawing blood and sailing on into the infinity.

I closed the bible and threw it at the door. It fluttered open like a bird beating its wings and slid to the floor. I tried to remember the names of all the women I'd ever slept with, or known or thought about. I imagined myself a woman—marching along the sidewalks in high-heeled shoes and a long mink coat.

The next day a guard came in and told me to get up. He led me down a hall between the cells; the keys jingled at his belt. A man with a long stemmed beard had his face pushed up against a barred window. His nose was red and bulbous, and one of his eyes was dead. He smiled without teeth.

We walked out into a bright corridor. We passed a checkpoint and climbed some stairs. An electric door opened and we went through. The guard sat me in a barely furnished office with no windows; there were bars on the transom of the door. A picture of the queen hung over a battered desk.

A key turned in the door; Jana entered the room. She was wearing a long black dress buttoned at the throat and an ermine coat. Her make-up was applied sparely, her hair was jet-black—rinsed of all the bleach—and pinned neatly on top. She carried a small pearl-trimmed bag in one hand and walked carefully on low gray heels. She looked like a wealthy housewife.

"I have arranged to have you released from the jail."

She pulled at the cuff of the fur and stared at the face of a thin silver watch. "Come, I will take you to the station. You must be out of the country in three hours."

My back was stiff, and all my joints ached. I rubbed my

thumb against the bone of the wrist. "What about the murder charges?" I said.

"Margo Bellini has made the confession. She said you had nothing to do with it. You are lucky I find out and call a lawyer." She narrowed her eyes. "They can hold you forever when they like."

I began to reply. She held a finger to her mouth. A guard accompanied us; we climbed more steps. I signed some papers; a man sitting behind a high desk returned my belongings. My wallet was a hundred guilders short.

We passed a final checkpoint and came outdoors. We crossed a drive and walked along a grove of trees. A Mercedes limousine pulled up alongside.

A chauffeur in a white suit took my valise and put it in the trunk. He opened the back door. All the windows were smoked gray and the upholstery smelled of roses. Jana waited for me to climb in. A glass partition separated us from the driver.

The car followed the river back into the city, past cranes and winches, past honeycombs of apartment buildings and vast concrete lots. We stared out our respective windows, without speaking; the scenes rocketed by.

I remembered a dream of a stadium, sitting in the highest seats, hundreds of yards above the field. I recalled another dream of a balcony, standing in front of a stained-glass window, watching the priest and the choir below.

I looked at Jana and she frightened me. I didn't know what she was, but I knew that I would never get closer to her, that her heart was buried beneath the sea. Her face was impassive, cold as ice; she stared through the window without presentiment of emotion.

"Are you with van Velden?" I asked.

She looked at me—her pupils were dilated, her lips were cold and narrow.

"This is not important."

The car slowed at a crossing. A pack of dogs ran across the road. A hay-wain passed before us.

"Do you have what you want?" I asked.

"What I want? ... No one has that." She threw out her hand. "This is only money ... It's trash and it's shit."

From her bag, she removed an oblong mirror. It was lacquered and painted with lilies. She tilted the glass slightly in my direction and applied some lipstick.

"You like me very much, don't you, Eddie?"

"I guess so."

"You like me inside."

"Something like that."

We went over a bridge, the tires bumped against stones, we passed under girders, the steel flashed in the sun. I held my hand to my forehead and tried to think of something else.

"Many things you have done for me, Eddie, without thinking of yourself. You are not a weak person—or are you only brave? Many are the weak who are brave ..."

I couldn't listen. The words bounced off my head, caroming against the cushions, shattering in atoms. I wanted to understand, but the sentences fell apart, the words bleeding from her mouth.

"Don't leave me, Jana."

She sat up abruptly, and dropped her hands to her lap. Something orange flickered in her eyes. "I never heard you talk like this, Eddie... You shouldn't say this thing."

She whispered. "Soon we are on the train, headed far away ... Leave this all behind."

I forced the words from my lips. "You're coming with me?"

She shook her head and raised her finger to her eye. She recoiled the lipstick and slid it into the bag.

The driver let us off near the main entrance of the Centraal Station. Jana said to him stiffly in German: "I will be back in ten minutes."

We threaded our way through the trolley tracks and queues. "Walk straight, Eddie, walk very straight. The police might be following."

A group of Afghan men were gathered at the mouth of

the building. They had dense, close-trimmed beards, and wore strangely colored clothes and tight-fitting gray wool caps. A scrawny girl in green leather rags was singing in a minor key through a microphone. A boy with his head wrapped in purple cloth sat next to her on a wooden crate playing an electrified mandolin.

I followed Jana through the doors and down the hall to the currency exchange booths. She pulled a few thousand guilders from her bag and pushed them beneath the plastic window. A thin man with spiked hair and a starched collar quickly counted the bills. He pushed back a currency I didn't recognize.

We stopped at a yellow board. The station was screaming with people and I couldn't focus on the names of the cities, the hours, the dates; all the numbers seemed the same.

"We must go to the gate eight."

We followed the corridor past a newspaper kiosk and went up a flight of stairs. We stood by the track, waiting. Jana lit a cigarette. A man in an orange suit drove a baggage cart down the center of the platform.

Jana turned her chin up and blew out a jet of smoke.

"Eddie."

"Yes."

"You are certain that Werner is dead."

I looked across the track. A girl in red and a puny sailor were holding hands. A puppy was caged in a slatted wooden box. The girl was crying profusely.

"He appeared to be dead. His skull was crushed."

Birds overhead landed on a beam in the roof and cackled. Jana held the cigarette between her thumb and index finger; she looked up at the clock. The last number flipped over, the signs whirled: Osnabruck/Hamburg.

"The train will be coming now."

"Where are we going?" In the distance was the light of the engine.

"To the northlands. The cold home of Loki, the cousin of dark Jana." She took a last pull off the cigarette and threw it onto the track. "To Copenhagen. Have you been there?"

"No."

She picked up her handbag. The train rushed at us.

"It is wonderful. The bars are open all the night and people embrace in the streets ... In the winter it is the best—it is terribly cold and the tourists are staying in their own fucking countries. It is very old, you can feel it, the buildings are strange, and not everything is perfect like here. The dogs shit sometimes on the sidewalks, and there are drunken people riding on the buses. People are laughing. Well—you will see ..."

A whistle sounded. We ascended the train. We walked down the corridor and entered an empty compartment in the first class.

Jana dragged the sliding doors shut. She dropped her handbag on the floor and pulled back the drape.

The train pulled out of the station. We wheeled past people tarrying at the platform, waving, smiling, weeping. We raced up to the man in orange, his luggage trolley swaying from behind like a caterpillar; we soared into a tunnel.

Jana pressed her face to the dark glass. "On the other side—is everything black, Eddie?" Her breath condensed around her mouth. "But no one can say ... Our millions of years—and we don't know anything ..."

She hung her jacket on a silver coathook and sat down on the bright green seat. Her complexion was pale and ghostly. I hoisted my valise up onto the overhead rack and reached for her bag.

"You must not touch it." She buried her face in her hands.

A spry conductor entered the room. Jana looked up and handed him the tickets. Her lips were parched and drained of blood.

He departed. Jana clutched her bag and got up. She seemed unsteady on her feet, unfocused, eyes drifting back and forth, as if waiting for something to leap from the walls. She pressed her face once more against the glass.

We passed the outskirts of Amsterdam. Church spires sailed by, green-black with age, octagonal apartment buildings, a soccer field behind a schoolyard. The buildings thinned, irrigation furrows ran in perfect parallel lines. There were greenhouses, orange and white rings on a crane, cyclists waiting at the train crossing. On a wall, graffiti: HUNTER KGB.

Jana sat down. "Close your eyes, Eddie. Until I tell you." I turned toward the window and closed my eyes. I heard her shifting through the handbag.

She touched my knee. When I opened my eyes, her face had regained its color; for a second I thought I saw an image of evil pass across it.

She got on my lap and my heart thrummed. I was overcome with her perfumes and the heat of her body, I forgot everything I ever knew.

She put her arm around my neck, and pushed her nose to my cheek. A wave of snowflakes began assaulting the glass.

"Eddie."

She nuzzled my ear, and toyed lazily with my collar. The snowflakes melted, plashing at the window and running in spidery veins along the pane. Her lashes slowly fluttered beneath the orbit of my eye, then stopped. Her hand dropped and she rocked slightly against me, as if she were about to drift off to sleep.

"Jana. Hey."

She caught herself and shook her head, pulling back her face and pinching her cheek. The snow turned to sleet and pelted sharply at the glass.

"What was I saying, Eddie ... I'm sorry ...maybe I need to take a cigarette...."

The train pulled into the station at Amersfoort. Straining, she checked her watch and furtively looked back and forth across the platform. A man in a wine-colored fur was carrying a megaphone at his side.

"I'm sorry, Eddie. I am stupid ... It is not like me."

In the corridor someone pulled at the handle of our compartment. *"Nee!"* said Jana sharply. Her eyes were half-closed; she scratched with her fingernails at her upper arm. The voices faded down the hallway. Outside, the platform was empty and it was growing dark.

"I have to sleep now, Eddie. Otherwise ..." —she rubbed her nose with the bottom knuckle of her thumb— "otherwise, I am lost ... You must wake me at Hengelo ... before the frontier."

Her eyes closed and she was sleeping. I watched her bosom heaving in perfect time; her face looked like it had fallen from a canvas by Perugino or Raphael. The train pulled out of the station; the snow had finished and there were clots of gray and pink in the darkening twilight sky.

I took a book from my suitcase and I read a story by Mérimée. The characters took on plastic identities, becoming things-in-themselves, their images glowed in my mind, cartoon, shining flesh. Before I knew it we were approaching the tiny station.

I shook Jana brusquely. She struggled to open one of her eyes. "Are we there?"

"Yes."

She shivered and pulled herself slowly up. She rubbed above the eyelids, looking fragile and helpless.

"Eddie. Listen. The German police come to look at the passports." She stood up and slung the handbag over her shoulder.

"Jana is dead now—no more. Do you understand?"

"I don't want to ..."

"Do you understand?"

I hung my head. "Will you be back?"

"Please Eddie ... you cannot make these ideas in your head." She put her hand on mine. "Do you really want to love ... you will love without making trades. Don't you believe this? Eddie?" Quickly she squeezed me and was out the sliding door. A window was open in the corridor; I heard the noise of rushing air as the train rolled away.

In a few minutes there were voices in the hall. There was a knock and a uniformed man with a gun at his belt entered the compartment.

He leafed through my passport, then compared me to the photo. There was a faint acrid smell to him.

"How long do you stay in Germany?"

"I'm going to Hamburg. Then to Copenhagen."

He sniffed at the air. Jana's perfume hung heavily. He pushed the passport back into my hand.

I stood at the open window in the corridor and watched the countryside flying past. A white-jacketed boy came down the aisle pushing a refreshment cart.

I bought a canister of coffee and drank it slowly in the compartment. We passed through the vast trainyards at Osnabruck and I looked through the glass. It seemed like the crossroads of the world, and the pain in my heart was too much to understand. A woman's voice came over the loudspeaker, announcing instructions for changing trains to Copenhagen and Berlin.

Everything was destroyed. I closed my eyes and waited for the waves of pain to end, and I knew they never would. I saw a collage of faces, women whirling like pinwheels ... I dozed off for a second ... I dreamed that I was slipping, I gripped the armrests tightly: the seat was falling through the bottom of the train.

A pink ghost of noise passed through my brain, derailing my reverie. I opened my eyes. I knew that everything would be gone.

Jana smiled at me, her eyes glittering. Her hair was bleached platinum, pulled tightly back, streaked with purple and zinc. She was dressed in black leather; a red silk ribbon tied at her wrist. She slumped down in the seat. I bit down on my finger hard enough to draw blood, and I knew it was real.

"Hello," she said. "Do I know you?"

"You must have me confused with someone else."

"With who is that?" Her voice came from far away.

"With someone who doesn't love you so much."

"That is a nice thing that you say ..." he turned her head and rested her cheek on her shoulder. "Say some more to me. I like to hear it." She closed her eyes. "What can you give for me?"

"Everything."

She opened her mouth, showing me the white tip of her tongue. "Go ahead," she said quietly. "Now it's yours, only for this minute, you must take it ... if the world is finished... if we can't see behind the curtain ... it will never come again..."

"I don't understand."

She gestured with her hands. The sleet strafed the window and the lights flickered. "Don't talk now, Eddie... Please ... Don't do this to me ..."

The train jerked and my bag lurched from the rack and crashed to the floor. Jana grabbed me around the neck, and pulled my face to her cheek. She gouged me with her nails and clamped her lips on my throat.

"Jesus, I'm swimming," she whispered. "I'm falling and swimming and falling ... Stay away ... the fire ... the black ... I'm falling, I'm falling ..."

I pushed my eyes against her forehead and I saw my sister's face as she pulled the trigger. I wrenched back and looked at Jana moaning. I lost my focus and she had three eyes, and four, and then she was a fairy queen with flowing petticoats, waving a magic scepter. Then I dreamed with her into the far other side, blue and automatic.

When it was over I pulled myself up and sat back in the seat.

Jana lay motionless with her eyes shut, only her lips slowly moving without producing sound.

"When I was a little girl, I saw you in my dreams... Now all my life is a dream ..." She began crying.

I attended to my clothes and hoisted the bag back up onto the rack. Jana rolled onto her side. The sleet stopped and outside huge factories were pumping smoke into the nighttime.

"Please leave me for a minute, Eddie."

I left the compartment and found the lavatory. I locked the door and washed up at the sink. I read the prohibitions printed in four languages over the receptacle ... *mentre il treno è fermato in stazione* ...

I dried my hands and threw the towel into a yellow receptacle. Another train jetted past us, rattling the siding. I unfastened the latch and pulled down the handle of the door. I pushed and nothing happened. I tried again, but it wasn't any use—it was locked from the outside.

Over the loudspeaker they announced the Hamburg Hauptbahnhof. I started beating madly at the door. Finally I heard a knock on the other side. I stopped the pounding and put my ear to the metal.

"*Was wollen Sie?*" said a quavering hollow voice.

"Someone locked the fucking door!" I yelled. "Let me out!"

"*Ein moment*," they said, and that was all.

The train slowed, the wheels changing their pitch. There was a panel of frosted window set in the wall, with clamps on top. I stood on the receptacle, pinched the clamps and tugged down. The glass came down half a foot and locked in place.

I felt my breast pocket and realized that my passport was gone. I saw that everything was going out of control. I found a narrow toehold on the edge of the casement and heaved myself up.

Suddenly I heard a woman screaming my name in a terrified voice. I pushed up on my tiptoes and pulled my chin over the edge of the opaque glass. There were hordes of people passing by and then I saw Jana being rushed down the platform by two men, one in an unfamiliar uniform, the other, despite an elaborate disguise, unmistakably 'Inspector' van Velden.

She was putting up quite a fight, and they each had two hands around her arms. They quickly disappeared from sight. I thought of trying to kick out the window, but then two more uniformed men appeared, their fingers touched to their holsters.

I lowered myself and sat on the receptacle. I was filled with a thousand feelings, and something rose in my throat, a glob of bile, or a part of my life, I couldn't say. It seemed like my eyes and nose were bleeding, and I raised my hands to my face; but it was tears coming down the skin in sheets, and the salt ran over my lips.

After ten minutes someone tried the door. There was a rattling of keys, and a lock turned: the door opened. It was an attendant, short in stature, dressed in a work-suit with a little cap. He was exceedingly well-groomed, his hair and mustache pomaded, his uniform starched and spotless.

He started speaking to me in a dialect I couldn't catch. I nodded and walked past him. I heard him turn on the faucet and begin to clean the basin. I went back to the compartment; the curtains were drawn, the door flung open.

Inside, the contents of my suitcase had been dumped on the floor. I picked through the clothes and toiletries. Everything was there except for my passport.

I went over the compartment inch by inch looking for a trace of Jana: a slip of paper, a hairpin, anything. Finally, in the metal garbage bin at the foot of the window, I found a tissue, balled up and smudged with lipstick. I held it to my nose and smelt the dying fragrance of her perfume.

I descended the steps of the train onto the platform. The Hamburg station is immense, as big as a stadium. I looked into the distance at the long row of arcades at the top of the stairways. Everything was cold stone, vaguely lit and covered with a smoky veil.

I walked toward the stairs. A voice behind me began crying insistently. I thought of running, but I didn't know where else to go. I stopped and stood frozen.

A small hand grabbed me by the shoulder. I turned with a dry mouth. It was the attendant, out of breath, holding an American passport. He waved it at me, beratingly, seemingly puzzled, upset perhaps, that I had ignored his shouting.

He handed it to me. His fingernails were manicured, the half-moons set nearly at the center. I reached into my pocket for a few coins. Insulted, he shoved his hands into his pockets.

"*Ich liebe dich*," I said. "I love you, sir."

He smiled like a child and we shook hands.

That night I walked down the Reeperbahn, the great garish red-light district of Hamburg. The sides of the street were decked with neon-lit strip clubs, casinos and shops of video-screen pornography; bars and nightlife of every stripe went on as far as one could see.

I turned into the Davidstrasse, a poorly-lit side street that was lined with prostitutes in unbuttoned fur coats and short skirts. Each one ran a line on me, spewing vulgarities and open invitations; several advanced and made grabs at my privates. It was tough to make a living in the cold months of winter; it was open season on men.

I walked through a wooden door into an arcade. A line of women were sitting on stools in a high window. They beckoned to me one by one as I passed.

I circled the police prefecture and strolled along a median. The clubs were more subdued, the lights like giant flowers. I found the Star where the Beatles played with Tony Sheridan.

I stopped under a street light. I gazed through the open door of a stand that sold doner-kebab and shawarma. Inside, lonely men were levering the skinless iron arms of slot machines.

Looking across the Reeperbahn, I felt that my brain was burning hot and cold from all the neon, that I was glowing first a midnight white, and then I was all the colors in the universe.

Some years later I was walking through the Tuileries in Paris, on my way to the Louvre to examine a certain painting of Andrea Mantegna. It was edging onto springtime and the groves of trees were beginning to show bud;

there was a magnificent scent in the air.

I approached a group of benches lined up along the walk. At the extremity of my field of vision, seated at the end of the last bench, I was sure I apprehended a familiar figure. I stopped myself a moment, to collect my thoughts, then approached the gentleman.

In his hands he held an old felt hat filled with breadcrumbs. He dipped into it every few moments and scattered the crumbs on the ground. A flock of birds gathered round him fought for the booty.

"Excuse me. Aren't you Lyndon MacBeth?"

The man slowly raised his head. His face was gaunt and lined, the eyes sunk deep into the sockets. His hair was cut rather shorter, with just a bit hanging on the collar. He wore a crumpled corduroy suit, slightly iridescent, and a white shirt open at the throat.

"Yes, yes," he replied thoughtfully, "I suppose so." He continued scattering the largesse to his tiny partisans. "Though no one calls me that anymore ... Do I know you as well, sir?"

A group of school children passed by. They were loud and unruly: the birds beat their wings and pulled back, creating a swirl of wind. Lyndon MacBeth waited patiently for the youths to depart; soon his flock returned.

"I'm Eddie Verlaine," I said. "I was once married to Claudia Lansdale."

He looked me over closely. He set the hat down in his lap and stroked his chin with his thumb, pulling it against the grain of a stubble of beard. He nodded and went 'hmm hmm.'

"Well, yes," he said, "I'm not sure I remember much of those days. I left the music world shortly afterwards, and then I was in prison for some time, and I've lost touch with those people ... Sometimes one of Trenton's solicitors will run me down and attempt to buy out my rights on the songs that we co-wrote ... I don't believe Trenton and Claudia remained together for such a very long time, either."

"No," I said. "She's in California—she does commercials and afternoon talk shows... And Trenton?"

"Oh—Trenton ..." His mind wandered off for a few moments. In the distance I saw a soldier mounted on a horse talking to a woman in a red dress. "He broke up the band after I left, and went on to a solo career. It was rather a failure as I've heard it. He had an adequate voice, but was entirely lacking in the fire of art—not that it always matters ... He only does production now, and shuffles real estate, and is worth countless millions ... such as he always dreamed..."

I stood at ease, watching as he continued feeding the birds. He attempted to dole out the remaining crumbs in as fair a manner as possible.

"There now," he uttered, when he finished. He shook the last smithers of bread out on the ground, and put the hat on his head.

"You see the birds, Eddie?"

"Yes."

"They carry God's thoughts with them."

I blinked and widened my eyes. "Is that right?'

"Yes it is," he answered. "Very right. I've studied them. In their wee brains they have radar systems that surpass the wildest creations of physicists ... Leonardo began studying their abilities in flight over five hundred years ago, and still, the clumsiest sparrow has more varied skills than any jet plane or space rocket."

MacBeth tugged at the sleeves of his jacket. He looked up into the clear blue sky and filled his lungs with air.

"See those flowers," he said, pointing to a bed of daffodils. "Why are they so beautiful?"

A light breeze passed over, and the daffodils rippled white and yellow. "I don't know," I said.

"Well, I shouldn't worry. No one else knows either." He rubbed his hands together, and his eyes assumed a curious gleam.

"Tell me," he said, "do you believe in the afterlife?"

A butterfly lighted on a bush abutted to the benches.

"Come again?"

"The afterlife," he repeated stonily. He leaned toward the butterfly and stared at it. It flew off and he straightened.

"I think I have to go," I said. I looked at my watch. "I'm supposed to meet someone at the museum at two."

"This is the afterlife, Eddie. It's right here—don't let anyone tell you otherwise. How could anything be better than this?'

"I don't know," I shrugged. "I guess you're right."

He rose to his feet and pliantly stretched out his arms. There was a purple mark on his temple that I hadn't noticed.

"Just the other year, two million humans, looking much like us, were slaughtered in Cambodia," MacBeth said softly. "Another million died of famine in Africa, many of them children who could not yet complete full sentences ... And yet, despite it all, you and me can walk through the Tuileries on a phenomenal day when the ides are not yet passed in March ... That's because we're in heaven."

He touched me briefly on the arm and turned to go. "Don't forget it," he said.

"All right."

He walked off towards the Champs Elysées. He had a slight limp, perhaps a souvenir of prison, and there was something sad about him.

"Wait," I said. He stopped and I walked up to him.

"Do you remember a woman named Jana?"

He turned around and stared at me. His face was slightly flushed. "Jana ... the gypsy?"

"Yes—if she was."

"Oh, I don't doubt it." MacBeth looked down at the walk; an earthworm was crawling along the cusp of the lawn. He shook his head. "She once saved my life."

"Did she—"

"Ask me no more," he said quickly. He shook his head again, and appeared deeply disturbed. He thought for a few minutes, scratching once or twice at his beard.

"I must tell you," he said at last, in a harried way, "because you've asked, and because—although—I don't know if I really believe in the supernatural ... I do believe in the unknown." He worked his hands together, and bent his head. A couple passed behind him hand in hand. One or the other was mute; they broke their grip and began tattooing finger signs in the air.

"What is it?" I said.

"I saw her just a few days ago."

I felt something bite at me. "Just a few days," he repeated almost dreamily.

"Where?"

"You must know?"

"Yes." I said.

"She was sitting on the stairs in the Opera, in front of the theater. I went up to her and asked if she didn't remember me. She said 'of course.' I asked her what she was doing. She said she was waiting for someone to come. I said something else, a trifle, but she wouldn't answer and raised her hand for me to stop."

It all came back to me. The years melted away. My tongue could hardly move. "And then?"

Lyndon MacBeth wiped a hand over his forehead. Although the day was too cool for that, he had begun to sweat.

"I went back the next day. I couldn't help it. She was still sitting on the stair. She looked up and saw me; she returned my gaze with black eyes, as if I wasn't there. I stayed awhile, and finally she raised her hand again, straight out extending her palm, telling me that I must leave. And so I did."

I thanked him, I'm not sure he understood why, and hurried for the Metro. I pulled two yellow fare tickets from my wallet as I began racing down the stairs. There was a throng of people at the gates. I pushed my way through, oblivious: no one resisted me.

I rode one train, it was the wrong one. I jumped off at

the next stop and ran along the walkway of the inter-change, my mind spinning in a dozen ways. As we pulled out of the station, I looked out the window and watched the people flying by like ghosts; we went into a tunnel, a light exploded overhead.

I took the stairs up three at a time. In the daylight, I looked around, confused, and nervous as a hare. I ran across the boulevard, jumping around the cars. When I reached the other side I stopped myself and closed my eyes. I stiffened my arms and took deep breaths, trying to get calm.

It didn't work at all. My heart was thumping, my mouth was dry as paste—my head was in flames. I opened my eyes and took long strides.

I don't know what I expected. I scanned the steps in front of the Opera House over and over, but there was no one there I knew. Just some people in small groups, idly chatting, a few pigeons and some crumpled handbills.

I sat down on the stairs and waited until nighttime. There was no sign of Jana. It seems like a thousand years ...